Fugitive Telemetry

ALSO BY MARTHA WELLS

FUGITIVE
TELEMETRY

THE MURDERBOT DIARIES

MARTHA WELLS

A TOM DOHERTY ASSOCIATES BOOK

NEW YORK

FUGITIVE TELEMETRY

Copyright © 2021 by Martha Wells

A Tordotcom Book
Published by Tom Doherty Associates
120 Broadway
New York, NY 10271

www.tor.com

Tor® is a registered trademark of Macmillan Publishing Group, LLC.

The Library of Congress Cataloging-in-Publication Data
is available upon request.

ISBN 978-1-250-76537-6 (hardcover)
ISBN 978-1-250-76538-3 (ebook)

Our books may be purchased in bulk for promotional, educational, or business use. Please contact your local bookseller or the Macmillan Corporate and Premium Sales Department at 1-800-221-7945, extension 5442, or by email at MacmillanSpecialMarkets@macmillan.com.

First Edition: April 2021

Printed in the United States of America

1 0

Fugitive Telemetry

Chapter One

THE DEAD HUMAN WAS lying on the deck, on their side, half curled around. A broken feed interface was scattered under the right hand. I've seen a lot of dead humans (I mean, a lot) so I did an initial scan and compared the results to archived data sets, like human body temperatures vs. ambient temperature, lividity, and various other really disgusting things involving fluids that happen when humans die. This was all data I still had in longterm storage. The comparison let me estimate a time of death. I said, "Four hours, approximately."

Dr. Mensah exchanged a look with Senior Officer Indah. Dr. Mensah's expression was dry. Senior Indah looked annoyed, but then she always looked like that when I was around. She said, "How do you know?"

I converted my scan data, my query, and the comparison results into a report that humans could read and sent it to her feed address, with a copy to Mensah. Indah blinked, her gaze turning preoccupied as she read it. Mensah acknowledged the report as received, but kept watching Indah, one eyebrow raised. (I was still using scan and visual to examine the scene, but I had a task group of my new intel drones circling above my head, supplying me with video.)

We were in a junction in the Preservation Station mall, a circular space where three small corridors met, one a short passage that led through to a large secondary main corridor: the Trans Lateral Bypass. (All the corridors here had names, a Preservation tradition that was only mildly annoying.) This was not a well-traveled junction, whatever its name was; it was mostly a shortcut to get from a residential area to a work area. (On this station there was no separation between transient spaces and longterm station housing like on stations in the Corporation Rim, but that wasn't even close to being the weirdest thing about Preservation.)

This junction, and Preservation Station in general, were also weird places for humans to get killed; the threat assessment for both transients and station residents was low anyway, and mostly involved accidents and cases of intoxication-related stupidity/aggression in the port area. In this specific junction, threat assessment for accidental death was even lower, close to null. There was nothing here except the lights in the high ceiling and the standard silver-blue textured wall panels, marked with some old graffiti and drawings that were actually being preserved as part of a station-wide history exhibit. I guess if you were really determined, you could find a way to get yourself killed by exposing the power connectors under the panels and shielding and, I don't know, licking them or something, but this dead human clearly hadn't.

The full station threat assessment for murder was sitting at a baseline 7 percent. (To make it drop lower than that we'd have to be on an uninhabited planet.) (I've never been on a contract on an uninhabited planet because if I was on the planet on a contract then we'd be inhabiting it.) You never found dead humans lying around on the floor like this.

"Well," Indah began, having finally finished reading the report. (I know, it takes humans forever.) "I don't know how accurate this is—"

Another security person walked in, one of the techs who normally worked on checking cargo shipments for biohazards, feed ID Tural. They said, "Our scan analysis says the victim's been dead for about four hours."

Indah sighed. Tech Tural, who had obviously expected this information to be greeted a little more enthusiastically, was confused.

"ID?" I said. The dead human's interface was broken so I couldn't pull anything off it. If whoever did it had been trying to conceal the dead human's identity, were they naively optimistic? Preservation Station kept an identity record and body scan for permanent residents and every disembarking transient passenger, so it shouldn't be that hard to run an identity check. "Known associates?"

Tural glanced at Indah and she nodded for them to answer. They said, "There was no subcutaneous marker or clip or augment or anything else with ID. We've done an initial search on recent arrival passenger lists using physical details, but couldn't come up with anything." At Indah's dissatisfied expression, Tural added, "Without an interface, we have to wait until Medical gets here to do the body scan so we can try to match it with the visitor entry logs."

Indah said, "And Medical isn't here yet because . . . ?"

Tural's face formed an anticipatory wince. "It's preventative health check day at the school and the bot who normally does the mobile body scan is busy with that? It has to move the mobile medical suite they use?"

Humans do the "make it a question so it doesn't sound so bad" thing and it still sounds bad.

Indah did not look pleased. Mensah's mouth twitched in an "I would like to say things but I am not going to" way. Indah said, "Did you tell them this was an emergency?"

Tural said, "Yes, but they said it was an emergency until the onsite medic pronounced the person dead/unrevivable, after that it went to the end of the list of non-emergency things they have to do."

Preservation has to make everything complicated. And that's not a metaphor for my experience here. Okay, yes, it is a metaphor.

Indah's jaw went tight. "This is a murder. If whoever did this kills someone else—"

Mensah cut her off. "I'll call them and explain that it's not an accidental death, and yes, it is an emergency and we need them here now." She looked toward the body again, her brow furrowed. "The council closed the port and deployed the responder as soon as we got the alert, but are you certain this person is—was—a visitor and not a resident?"

The responder was the armed ship currently on picket duty, discouraging raiders from approaching the station and rendering assistance as needed to local and transient shipping. With the port closed, it would be out there keeping any docked or undocked transports from leaving until the council ordered otherwise.

Tural admitted, "Actually no, Councilor. We're just guessing that they're a visitor."

"I see." Mensah's expression was not critical, but I can tell you the face she was making did not indicate that she thought Tural or Indah or anybody in the immediate area was doing a great job. It was obvious Station Security was out of its collective depth here. (At least it was obvious to me.)

Indah must have known that too because she rubbed the bridge of her nose like her head hurt. She was short for a Preservation human, a little lighter brown than Mensah and maybe a little older, but with a solid square build that looked like she could punch someone pretty effectively. That probably wasn't why she was senior security officer, which was more of an admin job. She told Tural, "Just keep trying to make an ID."

Tural left with the air of escaping before things got worse. Mensah's eyebrow was still aimed at Indah and it was getting pointed. (Not really. It's hard to describe, you had to see it.) Indah made a hands-flung-in-the-air gesture and said, "Fine, let's go talk about this."

Mensah led us away from the incident scene and out to the Trans Lateral Bypass. It was wide, with a high arched ceiling that projected a series of holo views of the planet's surface as if you were looking up through a transparent port. It was an offshoot of the main station mall, a thoroughfare to a section of service offices, with branches into supply areas. Traffic was minimal here right now, but a bot that worked for the station was out with a glowing baton, directing humans, augmented humans, and drone delivery floaters away from the junction entrance and Station Security's equipment. The group of security officers standing there tried to pretend they weren't watching us. Mensah's two council assistants who had walked down with us were watching the security officers critically.

The bot could have engaged a privacy shield but Mensah and Indah just stepped behind a large plant biome with giant paddle-shaped leaves that was screening the entrance to a food service place. (A feed marker in multiple languages and a colorful sign in Preservation Standard Nomenclature indicated it was called "Starchy Foods!!!" and noted that it was closed for its cycle rest period.)

It was relatively private, but I had my drones scan for any attempt to focus a listening device on us. Indah faced me and asked, "You have experience at this?"

Watching her via the drones, I kept my gaze on the Starchy Foods!!! sign, which had little dancing figures around it which I guess were supposed to be starchy foods. I said, "With dead humans? Sure."

Mensah's pointed eyebrow was now aimed at me. She tapped my feed for a private connection. I secured it and she sent, *Do you think this is GrayCris?*

Ugh, maybe? Right now all we had was an anomalous death with no indication of a connection to Mensah or any of my other humans that GrayCris might want to target. I told her, *I don't have enough data to make an assessment yet.*

Understood. Then she added, *I want you to work on this with Station Security. Even if it isn't anything to do with our corporate problems, it's a good opportunity for you.*

Double ugh. I told her, *They don't want me.* (Hey, I don't want me, either, but I'm stuck with me.) And it would be easier for me to investigate on my own, particularly if my investigations led to me having to do things like disposing of abruptly dead GrayCris agents.

(No, I didn't kill the dead human. If I had, I wouldn't dump the body in the station mall, for fuck's sake.)

She said, *If you want to stay in the Preservation Alliance, improving your relationship with Station Security will help immeasurably. This might lead to them hiring you as a consultant.*

Mensah didn't usually take the "this is for your own good, you idiot" tone, so the fact that she had meant she really thought it was a good idea. Also, I'm not an idiot, I knew she was right. But it wasn't like I could leave Preservation yet, anyway, even if I didn't like it and it didn't like me. My threat assessments were still rising steadily. (I had an input on my threat assessment module continuously now so I could get real-time updates instead of just checking it periodically, and yes, it was a constant source of irritation because it reacted to everything. No, it was not helping my anxiety. But it was necessary.)

Station Security had been briefed on the danger from GrayCris but I trusted them as much as they trusted me. (Surprise, it was not very much.) And they had no experience with corporate attacks. Their job was mostly accident first response and maintaining safety equipment and scanning for illegal hazardous cargo, not repelling assassination attempts. They didn't even patrol outside the port.

Indah watched us with an acerbic expression that indicated she knew we were talking privately on the feed. Mensah was still eyebrow-glaring at me so I answered Indah's question. "Yes, I've had experience with investigating suspicious fatalities in controlled circumstances."

Indah's gaze wasn't exactly skeptical. "What controlled circumstances?"

I said, "Isolated work installations."

Her expression turned even more grim. "Corporate slave labor camps."

I said, "Yes, but if we call them that, Marketing and Branding gets angry and we get a power surge through our brains that fries little pieces of our neural tissue."

Indah winced. Mensah folded her arms, her expression a combo of "are you satisfied now" and "get on with it." Indah narrowed her eyes at me. "I know Dr. Mensah wants you involved in this investigation. Are you willing to work with us?"

Okay, I'm not lying about having investigated this kind of thing in the past. It turns out the big danger to humans on any isolated corporate project, whether it's mining or—okay, it's mostly mining. Whatever—the big danger to humans is not raiders, angry human-eating fauna, or rogue SecUnits; it's other humans. They kill each other either accidentally or on purpose and you have to clear that up fast because it jeopardizes the bond and determines whether the company has to pay out damages on it or not. SecUnits are ordered by the HubSystem to gather video and audio evidence because nobody trusts the human supervisors, including the other human supervisors.

I had dealt with some instances of humans killing each other surreptitiously instead of, for example, in front of the entire mess hall during food service, but most had been pre–memory wipe(s) so the details were fuzzy. It was better to prevent them from murdering each other in the first place, by keeping watch for aggressive or destructive behaviors, things like trying to sabotage another human's life support pack or poison their water supply. Then you put in a notice to MedSystem to call them in for an evaluation, or reported to the supervisor who moved them to a different section so it would be someone else's problem if MedSystem couldn't convince them to stop. But whatever, the idea was to keep it from getting that far.

(And I know it sounds like they were all just running around trying to murder each other on these contracts but really, it was more like it had been with the poor humans on the transport I used to get to HaveRatton, who thought I was an augmented human security consultant. They had been complaining and fighting out of frustration and fear about going into contract labor. Actually being in contract labor just made it that much worse.)

I had archives of everything that had happened since I hacked my governor module, but I hadn't had as much relevant experience in that time. But what I did have were thousands of hours of category mystery media, so I had a lot of theoretical knowledge that was possibly anywhere from 60 to 70 percent inaccurate shit.

But Mensah was right, butting in on the investigation was the best way to find out if the anomalous death was a sign of GrayCris-related activity on station. I said, "Yes. Will you increase security around Dr. Mensah to the specifications I stipulated?" Yeah, that had been an ongoing argument.

Indah's jaw tightened again (she was going to hurt herself) but she said, "Of course, with a murderer running loose on the station, I am upping every security level, including those around the council and Dr. Mensah. I actually don't need you to tell me my job."

Oh good, maybe the security level would go from barely adequate to mostly adequate. I didn't make an expression because I knew Indah would be more annoyed by me not reacting than by me reacting.

Mensah cleared her throat in a "you are trying to annoy each other but are mostly annoying me" way. She said, "I assume an employment contract will be forthcoming."

Indah's voice was dry. "It will, no need to send the terrifying solicitor after me."

She meant Pin-Lee because she said "terrifying." Being the top Preservation expert in dealing with contract law in the Corporation Rim apparently made Pin-Lee like the CombatUnit version of a lawyer.

The employment contracts for Preservation citizens were pretty simple, because their planetary legal code had so many in-built protections already. (For example, humans and augmented humans can't sign away their rights to their labor or bodily autonomy in perpetuity; that's like, straight-up illegal.)

But I wasn't a citizen and also technically not actually a person, which made it more difficult. But Pin-Lee's contract would make sure that they couldn't make me do anything I didn't want to do and I would get a hard currency card out of it. (When we had first discussed the idea of me getting jobs as a way to encourage the Preservation Council to grant me permanent refugee status, I didn't know very much about the kind of contract in which I was actually an active participant. (My previous contracts were rental contracts with the company, where I was just a piece of equipment.) Pin-Lee had promised, "Don't worry, I'll preserve your right to wander off like an asshole anytime you like.")

(I said, "It takes one to know one.")

(Mensah said, "People, please. I'm scheduled to mediate arguments between teenagers on my next commcall home and I need all my patience for that.")

If I was going to do this, I wanted to get started so I could make sure this anomalous murder wasn't an indication of a threat to Mensah. Plus I had a lot of downloaded shows to get through. I said, "Can I examine the dead human now?"

Indah just looked tired. "Can you humor me and please refer to the victim as 'the deceased' or 'the victim' during the course of the investigation?" She turned to go, not waiting for an answer.

She missed Mensah mouthing the words *stop it* at me. (I guess the feed isn't adequate for all forms of communication, particularly those that involve a lot of glaring.)

Chapter Two

AT FIRST, PRESERVATION STATION Security had objected to my presence on the station. Correction, at first they were fine with it because they didn't know anything about me except that I was a security consultant who had retrieved Dr. Mensah from TranRollinHyfa Station, was injured, and was getting refugee status. Most humans, unless they get stuck working in an isolated corporate installation, never see SecUnits except in the media where we're always in armor. But Dr. Mensah had told the Preservation Council the truth (no, I don't know why, either) and then she had to brief Station Security.

(Senior Indah had been with the rest of the upper level security staff for the "hey, there's a rogue SecUnit here" meeting. You should have seen their expressions.)

There was a big huge deal about it, and Security was all "but what if it takes over the station's systems and kills everybody" and Pin-Lee told them "if it wanted to do that it would have done it by now," which in hindsight was probably not the best response. And then Mensah, Pin-Lee, and I had a private meeting with Senior Indah.

After some preliminary polite arguing between the humans, it became really obvious that Senior Indah was determined to get rid of me. She was trying to get Mensah to send me away somewhere, like a particularly isolated part of the planet, while the situation was being "evaluated."

I didn't even know how to react to that. For one thing, it was a terrible idea. Threat assessment for potential Gray-Cris retaliation suggested a steady increase, and I needed to stay with Mensah. I hate planets, but if she went to the planet, I'd go with her. (I really hate planets.) I wasn't going to the fucking planet alone and leave her here to get killed and let GrayCris rampage around the station.

Pin-Lee wasn't reacting, either, except to flick a glance at Mensah and send me a feed message that said, *Could you at least try to look pathetic.*

Yeah, I'm not going to respond to that.

Mensah didn't even blink. She said, calmly, "No, that's unacceptable."

Senior Indah's mouth went tight. I think she was angry Mensah hadn't told her about me as soon as we arrived from the Corporation Rim. (It had to be that, I hadn't done anything else yet to make her angry.) She said, "Just because you're accustomed to using a dangerous weapon doesn't mean it can't turn on you. Or harm others."

Okay, wow. But it wasn't like it hurt my feelings or anything. Not at all. I was used to this. Completely used to it.

Mensah was not used to it. Her eyes narrowed, her head tilted slightly, and her mouth made a minute movement that turned her polite planetary leader "I am listening and receptive to your ideas" smile into something else. (If she had looked at me like that I would have created a distraction and run out of the room.) (Okay, not really, but I would have at least stopped talking.) In a voice that should have caused an ambient temperature drop, she replied, "We're talking about a person."

Mensah can be so calm under pressure that it's easy to forget she can also get angry. From the minute changes in Indah's expression, she was realizing she had fucked up, big time.

Pin-Lee had a tiny little smile at one corner of her mouth. I checked her feed activity and saw she had accessed a station database and was pulling documents into her feed storage. Since she was human she was doing it slowly (it was like watching algae grow) but I could see the information she was assembling had to do with Preservation's original charter and its list of basic human rights. Also the regulations for holding public office. Public offices like Senior Station Security Officer.

Oh, maybe Indah had literally fucked up big time. Pin-Lee was planning a case for Mensah to take to the rest of the council to recommend Indah be dismissed.

(I knew by this time that on Preservation, dismissal isn't

as bad as it is in the Corporation Rim, so it's not like she would get killed or starve or anything.)

Indah took a breath to speak and Mensah said evenly, "Don't make it worse."

Indah let the breath out.

Mensah continued, "I'll agree to forget what you just said—" Pin-Lee made a sort of hissing noise of protest here, and Mensah paused to give her an opaque look that Pin-Lee apparently understood. Pin-Lee sighed and discontinued her document search. Mensah turned back to Indah and continued, "And I want to preserve our working relationship. To do that, we will both be reasonable about this and set our knee-jerk emotional responses aside."

Indah kept her expression reserved, but I could tell she was relieved. "I apologize." She also wasn't a coward. "But I have concerns."

So there was a lot of negotiation about me (always a fun time) and it ended up with me having to agree to two restrictions. The first one was to promise not to access any non-public systems or hack any other bots, drones, etc., a solution both I and Station Security were very unhappy with but for completely different reasons.

It's not like the private station systems were all that great; Preservation didn't use surveillance except on essential engineering and safety entry points. So it's not like I wanted to have access to their stupid boring systems anyway. If GrayCris shows up and blows the station all to hell, it won't be my fault.

Right, so it probably will be my fault. There just won't be that much I can do about it.

———————

So that's where I was, figuratively in an uneasy truce with Station Security, when Mensah had gotten the call that a dead human had been found in the station mall.

(She had pressed her hands down on her desk and said, "Could this be it?"

She meant the GrayCris attack we had been waiting for. Without access to surveillance I felt so useless. "Maybe."

Her face made a complicated grimace. "I almost hope it is. Then at least we could get it over with.")

And now I was literally standing over a dead human.

Tech Tural was back, and two other techs were lurking out in the Trans Lateral Bypass, running analysis via the feed and ineffectively poking databases. Mensah headed back to her council office, with her two assistants and the task group of drones I had assigned to her. Since there were no station cameras in the corridors (which, if there were, I have to point out, we'd know who had killed the dead human—excuse me, the deceased) I had sort of built my own surveillance network using my intel drones.

(I had promised not to hack Station systems. Nobody had said anything about not setting up my own systems.)

"No ID report yet," Tural was telling Indah.

Indah wasn't pleased. "We need that ID."

Tural said, "We tried a DNA check but it didn't match anyone in the database, so the victim isn't related to approximately 85 percent of Preservation planetary residents."

Indah stared at Tural. So did I, with my drones. Was that supposed to be a result?

Tural cleared their throat and forged on, "So we're going to have to wait for the body scan."

DNA sampling in the Preservation Alliance was voluntary and no samples were taken from arriving travelers. There were too many ways to spoof DNA-related ID checks so most places I knew of, at least in the Corporation Rim, didn't use it as a form of verifiable ID. Full body scans were more accurate, not that they couldn't be fooled, too. Example A: me.

Indah stared at me in a challenging "let's see what all you've got" way. Indah did not actually want to see what all I got so I just asked Tural, "Have you done a forensic sweep?"

"Yes." Tural didn't look like I'd asked anything strange, so I must have used the right words. Note to self: forensic sweep is not just a media term for it. "I'll send you the report when it's ready."

It was too bad they'd already done it, I wanted to see what it looked like for real instead of just in my shows. "Do you have the raw data files? I can read those."

Tural looked at Senior Officer Indah, who shrugged. Tural sent me the data files via the feed and I ran them through a quick analysis routine. There was a lot of stray contact DNA in the junction, caused by so many humans coming through here and touching stuff. (Humans touch stuff all the time, I wish they wouldn't.) But the presences and absences of contact DNA on the body told an odd story. I said, "The perpetrator used some kind of cleaning field after the attack."

Indah had just turned away to say something to one of the other officers. She turned back, and Tural looked startled. "You can tell that from the data?"

Well, yeah. Processing raw data and pulling out the relevant bits was a company specialty and I still had the code. "There's an unusual lack of contact DNA on the deceased's clothes." Samples from the deceased, the two humans who had found the deceased, and the first responder medical team had been included in the comparison file; the latter two groups of samples were present on the deceased's clothes, just like you would expect. But the deceased's own sample was not present. The clothes were as clean as if they had just popped out of the recycler or a sterilization unit. So therefore . . . Right, you get it. I turned my analysis into a human-readable form and sent it back to Tural and Indah.

Tural blinked and Indah's gaze went abstract as they both read it. That was going to take a while so I crouched down to look at the body's obvious wound. (There could be others, and this wasn't necessarily the cause of death; we wouldn't know that until they took the deceased to a MedSystem with a pathology suite.)

It was in the back of the human's head, near the base of the skull. All I could tell from a visual was that it was a deep wound, with no exit point. No sign of cauterization. And there should be more blood and brain matter on the floor plates. "If this was the cause of death, the deceased wasn't killed here."

"That we knew," Indah said, her voice dry. She glanced at Tural and said, "We need a search for what kind of cleaning tools could remove contact DNA and which ones are available on station. Particularly the ones that are small enough to conceal in a pocket or bag."

It's too bad we don't trust the SecUnit who is an expert at running those kinds of searches. Just to be an asshole, I said, "The tool could have been brought in from off-station."

She ignored me.

Tural made notes in their feed, then said, "Even without the contact DNA, the clothes should tell us something. They're distinctive."

You might think that. The deceased was wearing a knee-length open coat over wide pants and a knee-length shirt, which wasn't an uncommon combination as human clothing goes, but the colors and patterns were eye-catching. It might have been a clue leading to planetary or system origin, or at least suggest a place that the deceased had visited recently. But the chances were that it wasn't. I said, "Not necessarily. You can get clothes like this in the automated shops in some station malls in the Corporation Rim. If you pay extra, you can get whatever color you want and design a pattern." I knew this because my dark-colored pants, shirt, jacket, and boots had come from a place like that and I'd found it really annoying that the Preservation Station mall didn't have one. Most of the station's clothing supply came from the planet, where human-hand-made clothing and textiles were so popular there was hardly any recycler-produced fabric. (I told you Preservation is weird.)

Tural said, "I didn't know that." They leaned in with the scanner and took a tiny sample from the deceased's coat.

Indah's frown had deepened. She said, "So the clothes could indicate cultural origin, or have been chosen to blend in on some other station or system. Or just be a fashion whim."

Don't look at me like that's my fault. I'm just telling you shit I know.

Tural studied the fabric analysis report. "You're right, this is recycler fabric. It could have come from a store like that."

"Or a transport." They both stared at me. I said, "Some transports have very sophisticated onboard recyclers."

Indah pressed her lips together. Look, I know I wasn't narrowing it down, but you have to consider all possibilities. She said, "Can the clothes tell us anything?"

Well, sure. "The deceased wasn't afraid of being noticed. Or they wanted to look like they weren't afraid of being noticed. They wanted to look like a visitor." Humans from the planet wore all kinds of things, but on the station the most common were the work/casual pants, short jacket, and a short or long shirt or tunic, and the more formal long robes or caftans in solid colors with patterned trim. Bright multicolored patterns like this were unusual enough to stand out. "There are two ways to move through station transit rings if you're afraid someone's watching for you. You can try to fade into the background, which is much easier to do if there's a crowd. You can also make yourself look distinctive, like someone who isn't worried about being seen." I would never have been able to pull it off. But an actual human with actual human body language who didn't have to worry about the energy weapons in their arms pinging weapons scanners might. "You have to be ready to change out your clothes and appearance. You would always need to look like you came from somewhere else." Which was easy enough to do on big stations with lots of automated shops.

Tural's expression had gone from frustrated to thoughtful and even Indah looked speculative. Tural said, "Medical should check to see if this person's skin or hair color was altered recently."

Indah looked down at the body. "Hmm. If I saw this person swinging along the walkway, I'd think they were a legitimate visitor and not give them a second thought."

Uh-huh, and that's why I needed to oversee Mensah's security. I said, "You need a travel bag, too." It sounded facetious, but it really was important. If this human's distinctness had been a disguise, they needed a bag. A bag implied you had somewhere to go, it helped you fit in. I checked the images my drones had collected of the area surrounding this junction, but there was no stray discarded bag. "If the idea was to look like a visitor, there should be a bag."

"Can't hurt to look." Indah stepped back and said into her comm, "I need a check of the immediate area, and a station-wide check at lost-and-found depots. We're looking for anything resembling a travel bag." She paused to listen to her feed and added, "Pathology is here. We need to get out of the way."

Tural asked, "Can I take the broken interface for analysis? The scene's been scanned and position-mapped."

Indah nodded. "Take it."

Tural hesitated, glanced at me, but Indah told me, "That's enough for now. We'll call you if we need you."

I know a "fuck off" when I hear one. So I fucked off.

Chapter Three

MY FIRST JOB AS a consultant for Station Security had turned into a non-event, which was completely unsurprising. They really didn't want me here and whatever Mensah said, they weren't going to suddenly change their minds.

No access to private station systems was just the first restriction. The second was that I had to not conceal my identity. Not that I had been actively concealing it. Mensah's staff, family, and the council had been told what I was; it was just the rest of the station who either hadn't noticed me or thought I was Mensah's security consultant. Station Security had wanted me to implement a public feed ID and they had wanted to put out a public safety warning notifying Station personnel and residents that there was a SecUnit running around loose. Mensah had refused to consider the public safety notice, but in one of the stupid meetings with Indah she had asked, "What exactly would this feed ID say?"

It gave me a 1.2 percent performance reliability drop. I tapped Pin-Lee's feed and sent to her, *Make a legal thing so I don't have to do that.*

She sent back, *Mensah has to give them something,* but she sent to Mensah, *It doesn't want the feed ID.*

Humans and augmented humans can have null feed IDs. I knew from my shows that it meant different things depending on what polity, station, area, etc., they lived in. Here on Preservation it meant "please don't interact with me." It was perfect. And I'd already agreed not to hack their systems, what the fuck else could they want?

Senior Indah said, "The feed ID doesn't need to say anything other than what everyone else's says, just name, gender, and . . ." She trailed off. She was looking at me and I was looking at her.

Pin-Lee pointed out, "Everyone else who has a feed ID has one voluntarily. Consensually, one might say."

Senior Indah stopped looking at me to glare at Pin-Lee. "All we're asking for is a name."

I have a name, but it's private.

On their secure feed connection, Pin-Lee sent to Mensah, *Oh, that's going to go over well. When station residents are running into "Murderbot"*—

That's one of the reasons why it's private.

Mensah said to Indah, "I'm not sure we can agree to that."

"Frankly, I don't understand the problem." Indah made a helpless gesture toward me. "I don't even know what it wants to be called."

Senior Indah was acting like she didn't think she had made an unreasonable request. But the reason she was making it was that she didn't trust me and she wanted any humans or augmented humans who came into contact with me to be warned, in case I decided to go on a murder rampage. Because being warned by my feed ID would, somehow, mitigate being shot, or something.

Mensah pressed her lips together and looked at me. She sent, *Can you explain to her why it's a problem for you?*

I'm not sure I could. And I got why from their perspective it seemed like such a small thing. Maybe it was worth it to get this meeting over with and not have to listen to humans talk about how they didn't want me anywhere near their precious station.

For a name, I could use the local feed address that was hard coded into my neural interfaces. It wasn't my real name, but it was what the systems I interfaced with called me. If I used it, the humans and augmented humans I encountered would think of me as a bot. Or I could use the name Rin. I liked it, and there were some humans outside the Corporation Rim who thought it was actually my name. I could use it, and the humans on the Station wouldn't have to think about what I was, a construct made of cloned human tissue, augments, anxiety, depression, and unfocused rage, a killing machine for whichever humans rented me, until I made a mistake and got my brain destroyed by my governor module.

I posted a feed ID with the name *SecUnit,* gender = *not applicable,* and no other information.

Indah had blinked, then said, "Well, I suppose that will have to do."

That was the end of the meeting. Pin-Lee and Mensah hadn't talked about it, but Pin-Lee had stomped off to have intoxicants with some of her friend humans. And Mensah had called her marital partners Farai and Tano on the planet, and said she thought the future of humanity was pretty dismal, and they should take all the kids, siblings, their kids, and assorted relatives and move to a shack in the terraforming sector on the unsettled continent and start working in soil reclamation, whatever that was.

(I wouldn't enjoy it, but I could work with it. It would be a lot easier to guard her from GrayCris there. But Farai and Tano hadn't gone for the idea.)

Then two cycles later, someone had sent a photo of me to the Station newsstream identifying me as the rogue SecUnit mentioned in all those Corporation Rim newsfeed rumors.

There was little surveillance in the station but, at least before the agreement not to hack station systems, I had still been redacting myself from it. This photo had come from another source, maybe an augmented human's feed camera. It had clearly been taken after I had completed my memory repair, after a public inquiry about GrayCris that had been held in the large Preservation Council meeting chamber. Mensah was walking down the steps away from the council offices and I was standing behind her between Pin-Lee and Dr. Bharadwaj. We were all looking to the side, with various what-the-fuck expressions. (One of the journalists had just asked the council spokesperson if GrayCris reps would be allowed at the meeting.) (It had been such a stupid question, I had forgotten not to have an expression.)

Supposedly it wasn't Senior Indah or anyone else from Station Security who had sent the photo to the newsstream. Right, sure.

After that, Mensah, who was very angry but pretending not to be, gave me two boxes of intel drones, the tiny ones. (Indah had objected and Mensah had told her that it was a medical issue, that I needed them to fully interact with my environment and communicate.)

I think Mensah had already ordered the drones, as a sort-of bribe for me not continuing to point out that she hadn't had any trauma treatment or retrieved client protocol after what had happened to her on TranRollinHyfa. Indah didn't know that, right, so she thought Mensah getting the drones for me (giving intel drones to a rogue SecUnit nobody wanted around anyway) was Mensah's way of telling her to fuck off.

She wasn't wrong. Mensah's really smart, she can sort-of bribe me and tell Indah to fuck off simultaneously.

I did have other things to do besides watch for GrayCris

assassination agents and keep track of Station Security's attempts to shove me out of the Preservation Alliance. Dr. Bharadwaj had started the preliminary research for her documentary on constructs, so I had been to her office five times to talk to her about it, and she wanted to set up a regular schedule of meetings with me.

(Dr. Bharadwaj was easy to talk to, for a human. On the first visit, after the photo of me was in the newsstream, we had talked about why humans and augmented humans are afraid of constructs, which I hadn't meant to talk about and somehow ended up talking about anyway. She said she understood the fear because she had felt that way to a certain extent herself before I had stopped her from being eaten to death by a giant alien hostile. And she was trying to think how other humans could come to this understanding without the shared experience of almost being chewed up together in an alien fauna's mouth. (Obviously she didn't use those exact words but that's what she meant.)

The second time we had talked I had somehow just come out and told her that I thought being here on Preservation Station as myself, and not pretending to be an augmented human or a robot, was disturbing and complicated and I didn't know if I could keep doing it. She had said that it would be strange if I didn't find it disturbing and complicated, because my whole situation was objectively disturbing and complicated. For some reason that made me feel better.)

I had also been helping Ratthi with the data analysis for his survey reports, and he was trying to convince me that could be a job I could do for other researchers. Which, sure, I mean, it could. If I wanted to be almost as bored as when a lot of my job had been standing in one place unable to move and staring at a wall. It wasn't boring with Ratthi, but not all researchers were going to be so happy about the reports we constructed, or get me to go with them to live performances in the Station's theater.

But whatever, now I just needed intel for threat assessment so I could figure out if GrayCris had killed the dead human or not and go back to my happy boring life on Preservation Fucking Station.

I knew from my drones that Mensah was back in the council offices (I had a routine in place to check my various task groups of drone sentries every seventeen seconds). If the station had better surveillance, or if I had access to what little surveillance was installed in the transit ring, I could start an image search for the dead human, get a timestamp of when they arrived, and match it to the Port Authority's record of entry. Probably before Station Security managed to get the body scan from Medical.

It did seem unlikely that the dead human had been a GrayCris agent, because somebody had killed him. As far as I knew, I was the only one currently on the station looking for GrayCris agents to kill.

I just realized I don't like the phrase "as far as I knew" because it implies how much you actually don't know. I'm not going to stop using it, but. I don't like it as much anymore.

And speaking of not knowing things, I couldn't be sure the dead human wasn't tangentially involved in a GrayCris operation. He could have been sent by a rival corporate, even by the company, to shadow GrayCris activity, and been killed by an actual GrayCris operative.

Right, so while the corporate-operative-killed-by-GrayCris-agent thing was a scenario that made sense, there was zero data to indicate that it was actually connected in any way to reality. But the fact was, looking for anomalous activity is how you detect security breaches. A murder in a very non-murdery station like Preservation was definitely anomalous.

Unless the dead human had been here to visit other humans, they would have needed a place to sleep and put their stuff. Humans need stuff, I had never seen one travel without at least something.

Near the port was a large housing block for short-term residents, transients who were usually waiting for something: for a transport to arrive, for permission to continue to the planet or another in-system destination, for approval to become a longterm resident, other reasons.

Preservation Station didn't get nearly as many transients as the major hubs I'd passed through in the Corporation Rim.

Most humans who came here were going to one of the planets in the Preservation Alliance for a long stay, either permanently or for a term of work. The others were from outside the Rim, using Preservation as a waystation heading somewhere else, or they were traders or independent merchants with cargo transports. Occasionally there were humans from sites that were not part of the transit network, "lost" colonies, independents who had not maintained contact with transit stations, "lost" stations, whatever. There were no Corporation Rim corporations here, so no reason for corporates to come on business. Some came as visitors sometimes, but most were afraid to travel outside the Rim. (They thought everywhere outside the Rim was all raiders killing everybody and cannibalism.)

There were places to stay other than the housing block, like the hotel for longterm residents where Ratthi and the others who didn't have permanent quarters on the station had rooms. Where I sort-of lived now. Again, surveillance was stupidly minimal and without access to their systems ... permission to access their systems.

But there was another way to get the data I needed.

———

I went to the transient housing block first because it was statistically more likely, if the initial theory was correct and the dead human had been a recent visitor.

I stopped outside the entrance, near a seating area with chairs and tables, surrounded by large round plant biomes that were partly decorative and partly an information exhibit about what not to touch if you went to the planet's surface. (Yeah, good luck with that. Trying to get humans not to touch dangerous things was a full-time job.) I stood in a spot where I could pretend to be reading the hostel's feed instructions and sent a ping.

After 1.2 seconds (I'm guessing the pause was due to astonishment) I got an answer, and I went through the entrance into the lobby.

It was a round high-ceilinged space, with registration kiosks, lots of corridors leading off toward the room sections, and an archway into another room with shelves and cold cases where food products were stored for the humans staying in the hostel. (Or really, for any humans or augmented humans who wandered by. The Preservation Alliance has a weird thing about food and medical care and other things humans need to survive being free and available anywhere.) The bot was in there, restocking items from a floating cart.

It was sort of humanform, but more functional, with six arms and a flat disk for a "head" that it could rotate and extend for scanning. It had rotated it to "watch" me walk through the lobby, a behavior designed to make humans comfortable (its actual eyes were sensors that were all over its body.) (I don't know why bot behaviors that are useless except to comfort humans annoy me so much.) (Okay, maybe I do. They built us, right? So didn't they know how this type of bot took in visual data? It's not like sensors and scanners just popped up randomly on its body without humans putting them there.)

This is one of the Preservation "free bots" you hear so much about. They have "guardians" (owners) who are responsible for them, but they get to pick their own jobs. (Are there any who don't have jobs and just sit around watching media? I don't know. I could have asked, but the whole thing was so boring it might send me into an involuntary shutdown.)

It said, "Hello, SecUnit. What brings you here?"

Yeah, whatever. I said, "You don't have to pretend I'm a human."

The data in the ping had told me that this bot had different protocols from the ones in the Corporation Rim, probably because it had been constructed somewhere else. I identified its language module, pulled it out of archive storage, loaded it, and established a feed connection. I sent it a salutation and it sent back, *query?*

It was asking me why I was here. I replied *query: identify,* and attached an image of the dead human.

A non-dead human walked into the lobby, one of the hostel supervisors. He stopped, stared at us, and said, "Is everything all right, Tellus?"

(The bot's name is Tellus. They name themselves and hearing about it is exhausting.)

Tellus replied, "We are speaking."

The supervisor frowned. "Do you need any help?"

Since the bot was still unloading the cart with three of its arms, obviously he was talking about me. The bot said, "No help needed."

The supervisor hesitated, nodded, and then continued on down a corridor. I don't know what they think I'm going to do to their bots. Teach them to hack? Bots don't have governor modules like constructs and it's not like the Preservation bots weren't supposedly able to do whatever they wanted.

It's also not like I didn't know what the real problem was. I'm not a bot, I'm not a human, so I don't fit into any neat category. Also, I hate being patronized. (The whole bot-guardian system is like an attraction field for humans who like to be patronizing.)

Resuming the conversation with me, the bot said, *query?*

Because I could tell it was already running a search against its visual archives, I answered with a copy of the alert Mensah had gotten from Station Security.

It hummed aloud, surprise and dismay, another imitation human reaction. I would have been more annoyed if it hadn't also just produced a query result: an image of the dead human in mid-stride, passing through the door into one of the hostel corridors.

Hah, got you. *Query: room?*

The bot said, *query: ID?* It couldn't find the room assignment without the dead human's ID. Or at least the ID the dead human had been using.

I said, *ID unknown.* We were going to have to do this a different way. *Query: rooms plus target corridor = engaged plus without resident plus target time.*

The bot ran another search and delivered thirty-six results, all assigned rooms where the occupant was not currently present and was known to have exited the hostel before the dead human's estimated time of death. The bot added, *entry re: unoccupied maintenance inspection authorized. Concern: privacy. Query: item examine?*

The bot was authorized to make inspections of unoccupied rooms to check for maintenance issues and was implying I could come along, if I told it what I wanted to see, and if it didn't think it was a privacy violation.

It would be nice to look for memory clips or other data storage devices, especially if they were concealed data storage devices. But to make an ID I thought I only needed to see one thing. I told it, *clothing.*

Acknowledge, the bot said. It pulled its arms in and led the way toward the target corridor.

We checked seventeen of the currently empty rooms, and while the bot didn't let me touch anything, it did open the clothing storage cubbies so I could see the contents in the rooms where the humans hadn't left their stuff strewn all over the bed and desk. It didn't need to do that in the eighteenth room. It was fairly neat but the scarf draped over the chair was the same style of pattern as the dead human's shirt, but in a different color combination.

It could easily have been a coincidence, the style and pattern could have been popular and cheap at some transit station hub. And even with the image it wasn't actually a positive ID. But Station Security could make it a positive ID with a thorough search of the room and a DNA match.

I created a quick report with images of the scarf, the location of the room, and the feed ID associated with it (name: Lutran, gender: male), and the room-use record, which indicated that Lutran had been registered here for two station cycles. I included the bot's authorization to view the rooms, and sent it off to Station Security tagged for Senior Indah and Tech Tural. (Station Security was used to getting messages from me about their completely inadequate arrangements for Mensah's security.) I sent a copy to the hostel bot so it would know what was going on if they came to ask it questions. Then I signaled that I was leaving.

It followed me back through the corridors to the lobby, where a few new humans had arrived and were standing in front of a kiosk like they had never seen anything like it before. It went to help them, but sent me *query: next action?*

I still didn't have enough for a real threat assessment. I should go back to monitoring Mensah's security arrangements while lurking in the hotel near the admin offices and watching media. I didn't think I'd hear from Station Security again. (Or at least not about this; I figured they would come up with other ways to try to get rid of me.) I'd have to get intel on their investigation through Mensah's council channels. To get the bot to leave me alone, I answered, *task complete.*

I was already out the door when the bot said, *query: arrivals data,* meaning I should look for the dead human in the transit ring and its traveler records.

I didn't respond because I don't need a critique from a "free" bot and I couldn't access the arrivals data without Station Security's permission anyway, and fuck that.

Huh, I just thought of another way to do it.

It was annoying that the "free" bot was right, but I needed to go to the transit ring.

Preservation's transit ring wasn't that big compared to the major Corporation Rim hubs. Or even to the non-major Corporation Rim hubs. It had only one entry/exit point for passengers, near the booking kiosks where you could search for berths on the docked transports offering passage. There was another entry/exit point for crews of private ships and cargo-only transports in the Merchant Docks, and Dead Lutran might have come in through that section, but it made more sense statistically to start at the public entrance.

This being Preservation, there was a nice waiting area to one side of the transit ring's entry hall for humans to sit and figure out what they were doing, with couches and chairs and a mosaic floor with tiled images of the planet's flora and fauna, all tagged in the feed with detailed descriptions. Wooden conical structures that were duplicates of the first shelters used on the planet sat around, most of them holding information kiosks or displays for visitors.

I found a chair behind yet another plant biome (a big one, with reedy plants in a simulated stream) and sat down.

I had an ID that Dead Lutran must have used on entry in order to get a room assignment for transient housing. Finding the ship he had come in on could be an important data point. Based on the tech used to create his clothes, I was betting he had come here from the Corporation Rim and not another non-corporate political entity, station or whatever, but it would be nice to be sure.

I could hack the port's transient arrivals system but I had said I wouldn't, so I wouldn't. Also, it seemed pointless to do it just to run a search that Tural and the other Station Security techs could run as soon as they bothered to read my report. But just asking for information had worked really well the first time so I decided to try it again.

I leaned back in the chair, told my drones to form a sensor perimeter, and verified that my inputs for the constant cycle of checks for Dr. Mensah's sentry task group were all still open. Then I closed my eyes and slipped into the feed.

Transports don't hang out on the feed constantly downloading (not that there's anything wrong with constantly downloading) but they do access it to keep in contact with the transit ring's scheduling and alerts channels, and also to allow local feed access to any humans on board.

I had to sort through the hundreds of different connections currently attached to the station feed in the transit ring, humans, augmented humans, bots, bot pilots, small and large scale port systems, all interlinked and busy doing their jobs. Or in most of the humans' cases, wandering around. I was looking for the distinctive profiles of transports, which were different from any of the other connections. I could have done this a lot more easily by walking around from hatch to hatch and using the comm to contact each transport directly, but it would have been ridiculously obvious that I was doing something, even if the humans couldn't tell what it was.

(The humans not being able to tell what I was doing just guaranteed that whatever they assumed I was doing would be way, way worse than me having a brief comm interaction with each transport in dock, trying to get info for stupid Station Security.)

I found a transport connection and pinged it. It pinged back readily, with enough identifying information to class it as a passenger transport whose home destination was a small hub station outside the Corporation Rim. It visited Preservation on a regular route, carrying cargo and passengers, continuing on to five other non–Corporation Rim polities and then looping back home. Transports don't communicate in words (most transports don't; ART did, but ART was ART) so I wasn't really asking it questions so much as sending images and code back and forth. It had no record of Lutran as one of its passengers, and I moved on to the next.

This got boring very quickly. And it was the tedious kind of boring where I couldn't run media in the background. I couldn't code this process, each transport needed an individual approach based on its capabilities, and finding their connections to the station feed out of the confusing mass of inputs and outputs took more finesse than I was used to needing. I couldn't use a data range to exclude transports, since Lutran could have come in on any of them; some transports didn't require passengers to disembark immediately and Lutran could have stayed in his quarters on board for some time before applying for transient housing.

I also couldn't pull the transport's date of arrival until after I made contact with it.

And this whole exercise could be totally useless, if his transport was one of the three that had left before the body was found and the council had closed the port.

If I didn't find anything, this was going to be a huge waste of my time.

Possibly I should just stop complaining like a human and get on with it.

I had checked 57 percent of the transports in dock, when I hit an anomaly. I pulled a transport connection and pinged it with a salutation. It pinged me back with a salutation. (This is not how it's supposed to work, there's usually an answer protocol, even if it's in a different language.) But maybe the transport had missed part of the ping or had a different kind of protocol. (Unlikely. Ships from outside the Corporation Rim, particularly on the routes intersecting Preservation, had a variety of different protocols, some of them horrifyingly jury-rigged by humans. But by the registry signifiers in its feed connection, this transport was from a Corporation Rim origin.) I pinged it again. It pinged me back, still a salutation. Okay, I'm just going to start talking to it.

By poking around in its open feed, I found out the transport was a lower level automated crewless cargo hauler with booked passengers on the side. Preservation was self-sufficient and didn't import or export raw materials from the Corporation Rim, but did act as a cargo transfer point for other non-corporate polities that did. Talking to it was reminiscent of dealing with Ship, the cargo hauler I had taken to Milu and back, which had not abandoned me to die in space even though I wasn't entirely sure it had understood it was saving me, but whatever; it made me more inclined to be patient.

On my initial query, Transport tentatively identified Lutran as a passenger but I honestly couldn't tell if it was just doing that because it thought that was what I wanted to hear and it was trying to be polite. I backtracked and tried to get some more baseline data. What was its route? How many passengers, where had they boarded, and what were their destinations?

It sent me a garbled cargo manifest.

Uh. That was . . . not normal, not a lower level transport failing to communicate.

I asked it to perform a diagnostic and after five seconds got a stream of error codes.

I opened my eyes and pushed out of my chair, startling the group of humans at the opposite end of the waiting area who hadn't known I was there. My drones dropped down from their perimeter positions and followed me through the entry gates to the transit ring.

The weapons scanner (which I was not allowed to hack,

and which I wasn't hacking) alerted on me, but it had my body scan ID on the weapons-allowed list so it didn't set off an alarm. (I have energy weapons in my arms and it's not like I can leave them behind in the hotel room.) (I mean, my arms are detachable so theoretically I could leave them behind if I had a little help but as a longterm solution it was really inconvenient.) I was sure the weapons scanner would alert Station Security that I was in the area.

I took the wide ramp down to the embarkation floor, which was much less busy than usual. There were still humans and augmented humans wandering around, plus some hauler bots and maintenance bots, catching up on cargo transfers that had been ordered before the port closure. Some humans glanced at me but obviously didn't know what I was; the Station Security officer posted in the help area at the base of the ramp did, and watched me walk down the floor toward the transport docks.

(I hate being identified like that. I had gone to a lot of effort to not be immediately identified as a SecUnit, and now it all felt like a waste.) (I grew longer hair and everything.)

I had gotten enough info from the confused transport to figure out what dock it was attached to, and I confirmed it in the public access port directory. Nine minutes later I was standing in front of its closed lock where it was attached to the transit ring. I touched the hatch and pinged again. The direct connection gave me a sense of the transport's urgency that I hadn't been able to detect through the Station feed.

Instead of a ping I got a different garbled manifest file back; it knew the first file had somehow communicated to me that it needed help and it was sending the second to reinforce the message. Something aboard was terribly wrong, something that had left it with no way of notifying the Port Authority that it needed help. I don't think it had any idea what I was, but I thought it was relieved that I was here.

I needed to get onboard.

I also needed not to give Station Security any opportunity to fuck me over. There was surveillance on the embarkation floor, and I can tell when I'm on camera, even when I'm not supposed to access the system.

From my drone sentries I knew Mensah was in a council meeting now. I tapped Pin-Lee's feed to check on her but she was in a different meeting. I knew the others were on planet: Dr. Bharadwaj on a family visit and Arada and Overse at the FirstLanding university working on preparation for the survey they wanted to do, and Volescu was retired.

That left me with the human most likely to want to drop

everything and come watch me break into a damaged transport and the human also most likely to come watch me break into a damaged transport but only so he could argue with me about it.

So I called both of them.

Chapter Four

WATCHING ME TRY TO get the transport's lock open, Ratthi said, "You don't think we should call Station Security?"

I had my hand on the entry panel. The transport wanted to let me in but couldn't get the lock open. I was trying to force an emergency open through the transport's feed but the connections were inactive and it was like groping around in a giant bin of tiny broken drones for the one that was still intact. I said, "No. They told me they didn't need my help."

"Did they tell you that?" Ratthi said. His expression was doubtful. "What exactly did they say?"

I pulled it from memory. "They said, 'We'll call you if we need you.'"

Gurathin said, "I can't tell if that's you being passive aggressive or you being willfully obtuse."

I would be more pissed off about him saying that except a) he was right about the passive aggressive thing and b) he was standing where I had told him to stand, blocking the nearest port camera view of what I was doing.

Ratthi was on a rest break after finishing his work for the

last survey and getting ready for the next. I had been lucky to catch him on the way back after a meal appointment with his human friends. Gurathin didn't have any other human friends from what I could tell but he had been taking a cycle rest period, reading in one of the lounge areas with lots of plant biomes.

"It's definitely not willfully obtuse," Ratthi told him. He told me, "I do think we should call Station Security."

"The transport said I could come in," I said. "But it's too damaged to open the door."

"So we should tell Station Security—"

"It might be just a maintenance issue, which would fall under the Port Authority's remit," I said. I almost had it. "We won't know until we get inside."

Gurathin sighed. "You sound like Pin-Lee."

"No, Pin-Lee is much worse than this. And if it was her, she would be swearing at us by now," Ratthi said. He asked me, "I've always wondered, did you learn to swear from her or did you already know how? Because you two use a lot of the same—"

I finally managed to get the transport's mangled feed to trigger the hatch to open. I stepped back and pulled Gurathin out of the way of the port camera view, so whoever was watching could see the hatch wasn't damaged, that it had been opened from the inside. I'd managed to keep the transport from automatically triggering any station alerts, too. So even though it was me, we should have a few minutes to take a look around and pull info from the transport's systems before a human from either Station Security or the Port Authority showed up.

Ratthi craned his neck to see inside the hatch, but let me walk in first. "Are you sure no one's aboard?" he asked as he followed me through the lock.

I was not. There shouldn't be, but I hadn't been able to get a confirmation on that from the transport. I sent my drones ahead and said, "Stay behind me."

"This is ill-advised," Gurathin muttered, but he clomped along after Ratthi.

On visual and via drone cam I was looking at small low-ceilinged corridors, dingy and scuffed but mostly clean, worn gray and brown upholstery on the seats along the bulkhead in the small lounge we passed through. Lights were up, life support set for humans, but the transport was clearly designed mostly for cargo shipping with passengers as an afterthought. Ahead off the main corridor, my drones encountered a transport maintenance drone, wobbling in the air with its spidery arms drooping, beeping pathetically.

"Do you smell something bad?" Ratthi frowned.

Gurathin said, "Something's happened to the waste recycling."

The air cleaners were working but the filters needed

maintenance the transport couldn't perform. Or maybe it had stopped deliberately, hoping to try to alert someone.

The limping ship's drone swerved away from my drones and led them through a short upward passage and into the main crew lounge. Right, so this wasn't a recycler problem.

I followed the drones but stopped in the hatchway to the lounge compartment. Ratthi and Gurathin halted behind me in confusion. I had trained them too well to step past me in a situation like this, walking into a strange place, but Ratthi peered around my side and Gurathin stood on his tiptoes to see over my shoulder.

It was a fairly standard lounge with padded seats along the walls and quiescent display surfaces floating in the air. In the far wall, a set of steps wound up to the cabin area just above. On the floor in the middle were dried stains of various disgusting fluids that tend to come out of human bodies when they die. (I also have fluids that come out of me when I'm injured; they aren't any less disgusting, just different.) (But I also have fewer places for fluids to come out of, unless you count open wounds.) (Right, this is completely irrelevant.)

And sitting on the curved couch along the bulkhead was a utilitarian blue bag with a shoulder strap.

"That's blood, and—" Ratthi stopped as the realization hit him. "Oh no."

"Was someone ill there?" Gurathin asked, still trying to

see. (Note to self: tell someone to tell Gurathin his vision augments need adjusting.)

"Someone was dead there," Ratthi told him. He stepped back, worried and clearly upset. "Now can we call Station Security?"

My drones had just completed a fast scan/search of the transport and I knew it was unoccupied; whoever had killed Lutran—hopefully it was Lutran who had been killed here and not some other human we hadn't found yet—was long gone. The damage to the transport's systems meant there was no chance of retrieving video or audio without some extensive memory repair. There was nothing else here we could do.

I said, "Now you can call Station Security."

———————————

Station Security swooped in like they were a big deal and not hours too late to catch anybody, and made us wait outside the transport's hatch in the embarkation hall. It had taken seven minutes for them to arrive, and I had been able to collect a lot of visual and scan data in that time, including the download of the bio scan filters that Ratthi had suggested. I felt we had done a complete job, even with Gurathin distracting us by standing in the hatchway yelling at us to get out of the ship.

A bot that worked for the Port Authority had shown up before Station Security, pinged me, and then it just stood there. I'd seen it in the embarkation area a lot, and I'd never seen it do anything but just stand there.

(I had considered leaving a few drones hidden strategically around the transport to keep track of the investigation. But I had seen the thorough imaging scans they had done of the area where Lutran was found, and if the drones were discovered it would have been humiliating. I felt like I was at least one if not two points up on Station Security at this moment and I wanted to keep it that way.)

The initial response team was three Station Security officers and a Port Authority supervisor. They had taken a verbal report from Gurathin while eyeing me like they expected him to turn me in for whatever I had probably done. The first officer, feed ID Doran, said, "How do you know there's no one on the transport?"

Ratthi and Gurathin looked at me, and I said, "I checked the transport for possible fatalities and injured crew or passengers in need of assistance, as well as potential hostiles. It's clear."

The expression range was dubious to skeptical.

Gurathin made an exasperated noise and said, "That's what SecUnits do, that's their job. Why don't you do your jobs?"

"That's what we're here for," Officer Doran said, beginning to fluster.

I said, "Station Security Initial Incident Assessment procedures require one of you to view and verify the scene before calling additional assistance from the Major Incident Team, if the surroundings are safe." Not long after I'd first gotten here, I'd downloaded all the Station Security procedures so I'd know what I was dealing with. I added, "The surroundings are safe."

Ratthi had to fold his lips almost completely inside his mouth to keep from reacting.

"We know that." Officer Doran said to the Port Authority supervisor, "We'll go in. You wait out here." The Port Authority supervisor rolled her eyes and went to go stand with the Port Authority bot.

They had gone in, and after three minutes, came out again and stood around talking on their feeds. The PA supervisor started to set up a feed marker perimeter to warn off the hauler bots. The PA bot followed her around, which while not exactly helping, at least was better than just standing there.

Then Indah showed up with the same group of techs and officers who had been at the Lutran site. A second response team from the Port Authority, this one with more bots and different techs, showed up to mill around. Ratthi said they were here to assess the damage to the transport and try to repair it. (Apparently on Preservation this would be free? Gurathin said it fell under what they called a traveler's aid rule. In the Corporation Rim, the transport would have had to sit there damaged and racking up fines until its owner or an owner's rep arrived.) Station Security told the PA team to hold off, since the damage to the transport was evidence and would have to be documented before it could be repaired.

Gurathin kept saying we should leave, but I didn't and Ratthi didn't, so he stayed too, shifting around uneasily and occasionally pacing. "You don't think this is related to GrayCris, do you?" Ratthi had asked me after he had called Station Security.

"It's a possibility," I said. I explained my idea about Lutran being another corporate agent who had been killed by a GrayCris agent. "But without corroborating evidence, the threat assessment is undetermined." I could come up with scenarios where a GrayCris agent would have reason to kill another passenger on their transport, but without evidence I was just making up shit. (If I'm going to make up shit I'd rather do it about something else besides how a human got murdered by another human.)

"Then why was this Lutran killed?" Gurathin asked, his big brow creased.

"We don't have enough data to make a guess yet," I said, not as patiently as would have been required by my governor module. "There are too many factors involved, like did Lutran and the killer know each other before they boarded the transport. We don't even know yet if the killer was another passenger or someone who was invited aboard, or who managed to trick or force the transport into letting them aboard. We don't know how they moved the body from the transport to the station mall junction. We don't know the motive, if it was corporate espionage, theft, a fight, or even a random opportunity killing." We didn't know shit, basically.

Because this is Preservation, Ratthi said, "What is a random opportunity killing?"

"When a human kills another human just because they can." It's also the kind of thing that's much more common on media than it was in real life, but still.

Neither one of them seemed happy with that answer. I actually wasn't either. From everything I'd seen in the media, assholes who just like to kill other humans are hard to catch. But without more info, I thought it was more likely there was a reason that Lutran had been killed, and that it would have to do with who Lutran was and why he was traveling. Threat assessment agreed.

Besides, as soon as Station Security got off their collective ass, we'd—they'd have the surveillance video from the transit ring cameras.

Indah stepped out of the hatch, speaking to another

officer I hadn't seen before, with a private feed ID. Then she walked over toward us, trailed by the officer and Tural, the tech who had been trying and failing to identify Lutran.

Something in their body language made Ratthi step up beside me. It occurred to me Gurathin was maybe right for once and we should have left. It would have possibly been another point up for me, to send the report about the incident to Station Security and then be back in the hotel or Mensah's office acting like it was just another day by the time Station Security arrived at the transport. But it was too late now.

Indah stopped just out of what humans would consider comfortable conversational distance, looking at me. Then she hesitated, glanced with some annoyance at Gurathin and Ratthi, then back at me, with more annoyance. Tural was looking at Indah, and a little agitated like they wanted to talk and were just waiting for permission. The other officer was trying to do a stony stare at me but good luck with that, you need an opaque helmet to really make that work. Indah said, "Officer Aylen, this is . . . SecUnit." She didn't quite stumble over it. "And Survey Academics Ratthi and Gurathin, our other two witnesses."

Gurathin said, "We didn't really witness anything. I don't think we have much to tell you." Gurathin seems to hate talking to strange humans almost as much as I do. And he wasn't wrong, he and Ratthi hadn't seen anything that

I didn't have video of. But him talking gave me a chance to work around the privacy seal on Aylen's feed ID and see she was listed as a Special Investigator. I didn't know what that meant, but it was a good job title and honestly it made me a little jealous.

Indah was looking at me again. I hadn't said anything because what was I supposed to say at this point? Oh, I guess I could have said "hello." Well, it was too late now. Indah said, "I saw the report and I know how you identified Lutran as our deceased. We got verification from Medical on the body scan right after that. But how did you know Lutran was a passenger on this transport?"

Ratthi had shifted from acting defensive to acting like this was a meeting we were all having. He said, "So it was him who was killed in there, then? The person who was found?"

Tural said, "Unless it was spoofed, there was a DNA match. Spoofing isn't unlikely, but in this case—" Indah glared at Tural and they shut up.

I answered, "The transport identified him when I asked it. With its systems damaged it was unable to report the onboard incident to the Port Authority."

Tural was nodding. "The transport's giving us nothing but error codes. The analysts are going to try to do a restart but they'll copy the memory core so they can get the latest passenger manifest, and restore if anything—"

Indah gave Tural a "not now" eyebrow scrunch and they

shut up again. She asked me, "But how did you know it was this particular transport?"

"I didn't, I was checking all the transports." Then I added, "That's why it took so long." Yes, I was rubbing it in.

Indah squinted one eye. Aylen looked me over again in that way humans do when they're trying to intimidate you and they fail to understand you've spent the entire length of your previous existence being treated like a thing and so one more impersonal once-over is not exactly going to impress you. Then Aylen said, "One point I'd like to get out of the way. Did you have anything to do with this?"

Wow, really? I'm better at keeping my expression neutral after so much practice, but I was surprised at how pissed off it made me. Compared to a lot of things that had happened to me, you'd think it wouldn't matter. But here, now, for some reason, it mattered.

Ratthi made an angry snorty noise. Gurathin was grimly staring up at the arch of the transit ring's ceiling; they had both suspected this was coming, that's why Gurathin had wanted us to leave and then had stayed around himself when we wouldn't. I said, "No, I didn't. Why would I?"

Aylen was watching me intently. "I don't like having private security with its own agenda aboard this station."

Oh wait, she thought it was GrayCris. That maybe I had found out Lutran was a GrayCris agent and killed him, and now I was trying to lead the investigation along a specific path, using my two oblivious human friends as cover.

So, the problem was, that wasn't an unlikely idea at all. It was something I might have to do if I did find a GrayCris operative on the station. Which meant I had to answer very carefully.

There were a lot of humans lying to each other on *The Rise and Fall of Sanctuary Moon,* and I knew outright angry denials tended to sound incredibly guilty, even though they were often an innocent human's first impulse. You wouldn't think lying would be a problem for me, after 35,000 plus hours lying about not being a rogue SecUnit while on company contracts, then the whole lying about not being an augmented human and lying about being a non-rogue SecUnit with a fake human supervisor. But the last two hadn't exactly been failure-free; what worked best was misdirection and not letting myself get caught in the wrong place at the right time, and making sure no humans ever thought about asking the wrong questions.

Misdirection, let's try that. "I would have either disposed of the body so it was never found, or made it look like an accident."

Indah frowned, and Aylen's brow creased, and they exchanged a look. Eyeing me, Indah said, "How would you dispose of a body so it wouldn't be found?"

I'm not the public library feed, Senior Officer, go do your

own research. I said, "If I told you, then you might find all the bodies I've already disposed of."

"It's joking." Ratthi managed to sound like he completely believed that. "That's how it looks when it's joking." He sent me on the feed, *Stop joking.*

Gurathin sighed and rubbed his face and looked off into the distance, like he regretted all his life choices that had led to him standing here right now. On our private feed connection, he sent, *Or you could just show them where you were when this person was being killed.*

(Yeah, on reflection I think I misdirected in the wrong direction. It was the kind of thing a human or augmented human could get away with saying, not a rogue SecUnit. Even if they knew I was just being an asshole, I'd made them wonder, I'd put the idea in their heads.)

(And now if I did have to kill some GrayCris agents, I'd have to be really careful about what I did with the bodies.)

(It was probably better to make it look like an accident.)

I hated to admit it but Gurathin had a point. I pulled the right section of video from my drone archive. (I don't keep all my drone video because it would take up storage space that could be used for media, but I run an analysis of it for relevant stuff before I delete it. I was behind and still had the last 72 hours stored.) I clipped it around the relevant section and sent it to Indah and Aylen.

The clip was from one of Mensah's sentry drones parked

up on the ceiling of her council office. I was sitting on a corner of her desk and she was pacing. I'd muted the audio; her
complaining that Councilor Sonje was an ass was propri-
etary data. I let the clip run, showing I'd had an alert from
another sentry drone, warned Mensah, and got off her desk
in time to be standing by the wall when Councilor Ephraim
walked in. Then I stopped the clip.

So that was one planetary leader plus one councilor who
had seen me at the council offices across the station when
Lutran was being killed.

Indah sighed (yes, she did that a lot around me) and
said, "Continue, Officer Aylen."

Aylen said, "The reason I had to ask was this," and via
the feed she sent me a video clip.

It was the video from the transit ring surveillance camera. The clip had been processed already but the timestamp
was intact. It showed the transport's lock, and Lutran
walking up to it, asking for entrance, and being admitted.
The hatch closed after him. I fast-forwarded through the
video, but there was nothing else. No one else approached
the transport's hatch, no one had entered the transport after Lutran. I said, "There was someone already in there?"

My drones showed me Aylen's grim expression. "No. No
one other than Lutran ever entered or exited that transport."

It had to be a hack. It wasn't like the way I removed
myself from video surveillance—I did that from inside the

system, removing the images of me and substituting images taken before or after I walked into view. It was nearly seamless, but it was easier to spot than this. The person who had done this had known the video might be checked by humans, not just a monitoring system.

If it was a person. Could GrayCris have sent another SecUnit? Or a CombatUnit?

My organic skin actually had a prickling reaction like from sudden exposure to cold air. Could they afford that kind of firepower just for revenge? I checked Mensah's drones, and tightened the drone sentry perimeter around the admin office block anyway. I didn't want to scare her with something that might just be me being nervous.

(Ratthi was asking Indah, "Can I see too?"

"No," she told him.)

I pulled the clip apart to look at its underlying code, but it didn't tell me anything. Aylen said, "From the report on how you rescued Dr. Mensah from the corporate station, you can do something similar?"

I said, "I can, but only under certain circumstances." Circumstances which I am not going to explain to you, Special Investigator. "Is your security system compromised?" It was kind of an urgent question.

Indah was watching me closely. "Our analysts say the PA's system hasn't been hacked. They think it could be a jamming device."

Which was good, because that meant it wasn't a construct. A construct would use a hack, not a tool. "I don't know of anything that could do that." I started a search against my own archives, which included the tech catalogs I'd used to pick out the new drones Dr. Mensah had bought for me. "And the Corporation Rim runs on surveillance, there's no way a tool like this wouldn't be banned there. At least, banned for commercial sale." My search wasn't finding any results. The only jamming devices I'd seen like this were in the media, secret weapons or magical artifacts. "It might come from outside the Rim."

"So it would be an espionage tool." Aylen glanced at Indah, who looked grim.

I started to say that they never used SecUnits for espionage, and then realized I didn't actually know that for sure. Take away our armor and alter our appearance and give us the right module . . .

There was a lot I didn't know for sure.

I am going to have to stop scaring the shit out of myself.

I asked, "Did they use this when they removed the body from the transport?"

"No." Aylen sent me another clip. "A simpler method."

On this video there was no attempt to hide what was happening. A floating delivery cart arrived, and the transport's hatch opened to let it in. Seven minutes later, the hatch opened again and the cart floated out. Well, that sucked because it was so obvious. It looked like a standard large cart, a three-meter square box used for deliveries around the port. I said, "The subject is in the cart with the body. Who called for the cart?"

Aylen said, "We're looking for the cart now. But it's likely the perpetrator would have cleaned it. We already know they have access to a sterilizer to remove contact DNA. And it's unlikely they used their own ID to request it."

This sucks more. All you needed to get a cart was an address, and the subject could have used the transport's lock ID.

Gurathin said, "Then why didn't this person clean the transport? If they had, we wouldn't have known this was where what's his name was killed. We'd know the transport was damaged, that was all."

It was a good question and I had a good answer. "They meant to. They thought they had more time to come back."

Indah made a thoughtful noise. Aylen was still eyeing me like she suspected something. Then Indah shook her head and said, "Forensics and Medical are going to need this scene for a while. Investigator, what's your next step?"

Aylen wasn't caught unprepared. "We can't locate this transport's contractor yet, but we have the ID of the outsystem ship that was supposed to deliver its next cargo. I'm going to the private dock to speak to them."

"Outsystem" on Preservation meant the same thing as

what the Corporation Rim called "non-corporate political entities," which were basically planetary settlements, stations, moons, floating rocks, whatever that were not under corporate ownership. They might be nice like Preservation or total shitshows, you never knew.

Indah said, "Good. Take SecUnit."

Yeah, I was surprised too.

Chapter Five

AYLEN MADE IT CLEAR Ratthi and Gurathin were not invited, which was fine, since Gurathin didn't want to go and Ratthi was glad because he thought this meant that Station Security knew I didn't have anything to do with Lutran's death. Aylen did not make it clear that she didn't like the fact that I was invited. It would have been easier if she had, because then I would have known where I stood, and if I should be an asshole or not.

Followed by two Station Security officers (feed IDs Farid and Tifany), the Port Authority supervisor (feed ID Gamila), and the Port Authority bot, we walked over to the end of the public docks, through the gates into the cargo section. I did a quick search on Preservation's local (public) newsstream archive, and found out that Aylen's title meant she was called on by Preservation authorities to investigate stuff they couldn't figure out, both on the station and down on the planet. She also did family and workplace arbitration, which meant a lot of talking to upset humans. So, not as cool a job as the title implied.

PA Supervisor Gamila had been pulling info into her

feed, and now said, "This cargo transfer has been on hold for two cycles. We were waiting for an authorization but it hadn't shown up yet when the order to close the port came through."

Aylen asked her, "Do you know why?"

"No idea. The ship, the *Lalow,* isn't responding to messages." Gamila sounded annoyed. "It doesn't use modules, and there's no record of the cargo being offloaded, so we assume it's still aboard."

Aylen didn't react but my drones saw Farid and Tifany exchange significant looks. They weren't wrong; we already had one dead human associated with this ship, there was a 42 percent chance the *Lalow*'s failure to respond meant something more suspicious than ignoring their Port Authority feed messages.

The cargo section of the Merchant Docks wasn't that different from the Public Docks. There was the big space of the embarkation hall with a line of sealed docking hatches against the far bulkhead. Big cargo bots (the configuration that usually only lived on the outside hulls of stations and hauled transport-sized modules) were sitting around or hanging, dormant, from the curve of the high ceiling. The low-level specialized lifters were parked and only a scatter of humans and augmented humans wandered the stacks of pressurized containers. Large modules were pushed back against the bulkhead, waiting to be loaded and shoved out the module drop so they could be attached to transports. Most of the ships currently in dock didn't use modules, they had cargo compartments that had to be unloaded through inconvenient specialized hatches. That wasn't unusual for an outsystem/non-corporate political entity ship.

Preservation has high safety standards so we passed through two air walls before we got to the cargo ship's hatch. (High safety standards are great when they're designed to protect humans against dangerous stuff like hatch failures and hull breaches; when they're designed to protect humans against rogue SecUnits, not so much.)

I tried a ping but only got a response from the ship's transit ring–assigned marker, which had its docking number and the *Lalow* registry name. This meant no bot pilot that I could get information from. That was depressing. I had no idea what else I was supposed to do as a member of this group and just following humans around listening to them talk felt a lot like just being a SecUnit again. I mean, I am a SecUnit, but . . . You know what I mean.

Aylen tapped the ship's comm for attention and sent her feed ID, and added, "I'm a Special Investigator for Station Security. I'm here with a Port Authority supervisor. We need to speak to you about the transport contracted to your trading concern, the one currently in dock in the public transport ring. It's urgent."

I'd stopped out of view of the hatch cam, standing to one side, because that's what SecUnits do. The PA bot came over and stood next to me. Great, that's great. I wondered if it did anything that wasn't related to standing around.

The comm acknowledgment pinged and a voice, echoing with the feed-assisted translation, replied, "Just you and the PA. Leave the port heels outside."

I wonder what the original word choice was that the feed's translation algorithm had decided "heels" was a good equivalent in Preservation Standard.

(I wasn't the only one wondering. Tifany's eyes narrowed and Farid mouthed the word "heels" slowly.)

Aylen glanced at Gamila, and told the officers, and me and the bot I guess, "Wait here."

The hatch slid open and as they stepped toward it, my threat assessment module spiked.

I checked my drone inputs from Mensah's task group first, even though they had reported in on schedule, eleven seconds ago, but they were all nominal. Mensah was still in the council offices, the big meeting having broken up into little meetings. She was sitting with four other councilors going over feed documents while they had cups of one of the hot liquids humans like.

Aylen and Gamila had just walked through the hatch, which was now sliding shut. I had the impulse to lunge forward and stop it, but I didn't, because I didn't want to look more like a rogue SecUnit than I already did.

And the hatch sealed. Oh, Murderbot, I think you just made a mistake.

Farid cleared his throat. "So . . . you're really a SecUnit?"

Yeah, I get that a lot here. I said, "Are you on the feed with Aylen?" She might have a private connection with the two officers that I wasn't included on.

"Not right now." Farid's brow creased and his gaze went to the hatch. "Balin, are you on with Supervisor Gamila?"

Who the fuck is—Oh, it's the bot. Balin tilted its head and said, "No, Officer."

Tifany gripped her baton and shifted uneasily.

This is the other thing. Station Security isn't armed except with those extendable batons (they don't even deliver shocks, they're just for hitting/holding off aggressive intoxicated humans) and the officers are only issued energy weapons when there's actually an energy-weapon-involved emergency. Which is good, because the fewer humans running around with weapons the better. (I say that as a SecUnit who has been shot a lot, often by my own clients, accidentally and on purpose.) But it also meant Aylen was in there unarmed.

I tried to secure a connection with Aylen or Gamila. No response. I tried a test message, a ping that would bounce off the ship's comm or feed, and got nothing. Which meant something was jamming me, something that had been activated since the hatch had closed.

Fuck not hacking systems. I hit the port admin feed and connected to SafetyMonitor, the PA system that kept up a constant connection with all ships and transports in dock. I used it to find and break the ship's secure connection to the feed, and tried to pull camera views from inside, but I couldn't find any video connections except the stupid hatch camera. I caught an audio source but all I could hear was humans yelling some distance away; they must be in another part of the ship, away from the audio pick-up. I found Aylen's connection to the port feed and upped it, trying to get through to her.

I upped it enough that I caught a burst of static from her and relayed it to the Station Security feed. Both Tifany and Farid looked startled and Balin the bot expanded a sensor net from the back of its neck. I stripped out the static; it was Aylen's ID, and she was sending a Station Security urgent assistance code.

For fuck's sake, I knew this was a bad idea and I stood here like an idiot and let it happen. I turned to Tifany and Farid. "I need to get in there."

Farid had a hand on his interface, sending another urgent-assistance-needed code to the Station Security comm. Tifany was more direct. She drew her baton and said, "Balin, get us inside."

The PA bot stood up to twice my height (I honestly hadn't realized it had been crouching until that point), extended an arm, shoved spidery fingers into the control interface in the bulkhead next to the hatch, and sent a complex ping I realized was a decoder. The hatch slid open.

Okay, so that was what the PA bot did when it wasn't just standing around.

My drones zipped past me and I dove through the hatch after them. This is what I do when I'm not standing around.

Past the airlock, I had a drone view of a shabby corridor, an open hatch at the end, and a shabby human/Target One standing there with a big energy weapon. Audio picked up angry human shouting. Past the target and the hatch was a large compartment with three corridors leading off it. Aylen and Gamila were backed into a corner, Aylen in front with her arms out, trying to shield Gamila. Four additional targets, two armed, faced them. Target Two was the closest, aiming a projectile weapon at them and yelling. Target Three: initial assessment = most likely to fire. She was further away from the hostages, also yelling, and waving her projectile weapon.

Warned by the hatch opening, Target One had time to turn toward me and lift the weapon. I had two humans trying to come in behind me so I didn't dodge, but I didn't want to block the energy burst with my head, either. I fired from my right arm and hit the Target's weapon. (I could have aimed for his face but I didn't consider him that much of a threat.) He yelped and spun sideways as I reached him. I bonked his head against the edge of the hatch and yanked the damaged weapon away.

I flung him through the hatch in front of me to draw fire, and then stepped through to throw the broken weapon at Armed Target Two. It bounced off her head as I fired my left arm weapon at Armed Target Three and hit her in the chest and shoulder. I was still moving across the compartment and I slammed into Unarmed Target Four along the way and threw him into Target Two who had stumbled back and dropped her weapon. They both went down in a heap and I slid to a stop with my back to Aylen and Gamila. I had my drone task group do a fast circuit of the compartment then break into small squads. Three squads took up sentry positions and the rest shot out of the hatches to search the ship for more targets.

Not an ideal intervention/retrieval; my speed had been a little low. Trying to keep Tifany and Farid from getting shot had thrown me off. Also, I wasn't sure yet if the Targets were hostiles or just really stupid, so I had held back a little. Target Three had crumpled to the floor, still conscious and trying to grope for her weapon. Before I had to shoot her again, Tifany and Farid barreled in and Farid scooped up the weapon. Targets One and Four were dazed and not attempting to move, Target Five had dropped to the floor and was screaming for no reason. Target Two sprawled on the floor, pretending to be unconscious.

I would have worried about an as yet unknown Target trying to lock us inside (it wouldn't have worked, but it would have been annoying to deal with) (nobody wants to be locked in a ship with an annoyed SecUnit) (nobody) but my sentry drones had a camera view of Balin planting itself in the hatchway and extending four bracing limbs to keep it open. (I'm guessing the Port Authority has dealt with problem crews before.)

Tifany moved further into the room, taking up a guard position to my left as Farid said, "We've called for assistance, and uh, I'll alert Medical."

I was getting drone video telling me that the ship was a stripped-down cargo hauler, with a small livable space. The drones hadn't found any other occupants. From inside, the jamming was easy to take down, and I pulled a manifest from the ship's feed to double-check the complement. I said, "Ship is clear, listed crew is accounted for." Because I was tired of Target Two's shit, I turned around to ask Aylen and Gamila, "Are you injured?"

Target Two made a wild grab for her fallen projectile weapon. I kicked the weapon over to Tifany, who snatched it up and secured it. (Yes, it was unnecessary and showing off.)

Aylen said, "We're unhurt." She sounded calm, a dry

edge to her voice, but her forehead was damp with sweat and her heart rate was still elevated. Her jacket and shirt had been disarranged, like someone had grabbed her and pushed her. "Thank you for intervening."

Gamila leaned against the wall, a hand pressed to her chest. "I'm not even sure what happened! They threatened us, wouldn't even listen to why we were here."

"You're here to take our ship!" Target Two snarled, the feed translating. "You pussing corporates! You sent a Sec-Unit after us!"

I turned to look down at her. "You didn't know they had a SecUnit until we broke in. Try again."

Target Two's brow knit as she looked up at me and her mouth hung open.

Target Five moaned, "Shut up, Fenn. They're going to take our ship."

Aylen shook her head wearily and Gamila said, "You should have thought of that before you attacked us!"

My drone sentries saw the Station Security Response Team thunder up to the outer hatch. Balin unwedged itself from its guard position, strode down the corridor, and folded itself down to get into the compartment. It extended a limb across to Gamila, she took it, and it led her out of the ship.

Nobody moved until they were out of the way. Then the response team crowded in and Aylen said, "Arrest everyone associated with this ship. They obviously don't want to talk to us here, so we'll do it at the station."

———————

Putting it mildly, it was weird to voluntarily walk into a Station Security office.

I had never been to one before on any station. (If I had, I'd be parts and recycler trash and you wouldn't be reading this.) SecUnits weren't normally used in stations in the Corporation Rim, and we sure weren't used in normal station regulation enforcement. We were only deployed on a station as an extreme measure, like repelling a raider attack. (And stations with deployment centers weren't likely to be attacked anyway, unless there were an absolute shit-ton of raiders or they were really stupid or both.) Palisade Security, working for GrayCris, had used a SecUnit as part of their hostage security team on TranRollinHyfa because they were worried about me showing up. And they had used two SecUnits and a CombatUnit as fugitive pursuit when I escaped with Mensah. And look how that had turned out for them.

But anyway, for most of my career as an escaped rogue SecUnit, staying away from Station Security had been kind of important.

Preservation's Station Security office was next to the Port Authority, part of the barrier that separated the port's embarkation area from the rest of the station. Both offices had entrances into the admin section of the mall and the transit ring.

Not long after I had first gotten here I had accessed a map of the security office interior from the station archives. The first level was a public area, where humans came in to complain about each other and to pay fines for cargo and docking violations. (Preservation had two economies, one a complicated barter system for planetary residents and one currency-based for visitors and for dealing with other polities. Most of the humans here didn't really understand how important hard currency was in the Corporation Rim but the council did, and Mensah said the port took in enough in various fees to keep the station from being a drain on the planet's resources.) The second level was much bigger and had work spaces, conference rooms, and accident/safety equipment storage. There was also a separate attached space for holding cells, and a larger separate section for storing and analyzing samples from potentially hazardous cargo, and a small medical treatment area that seemed to be mostly used for intoxicated detainees.

The response team brought in the detainees through the transit ring entrance. Targets Two and Three had already come in on gurneys headed for the medical area but the others were mostly ambulatory.

The weapons scanners on the station's entrance went off on me, of course.

It caused some confusion, because the response team thought someone had screwed up and not searched the detainees properly. I stood there for two minutes and twelve seconds wondering if anyone would figure it out while they searched the detainees again, looking for the weapon the scanner was alerting on. In their defense, they had actually done the weapons search right the first time (I had verified it with scan and visual), and they had confiscated the detainees' interfaces. (None of them were augmented humans—apparently it wasn't common to be feed augmented in the polities outside the Corporation Rim that used Preservation as a waystation.) But not so much in their defense, they had forgotten a SecUnit was standing behind them.

Finally I pulled up my sleeve (using my onboard energy weapons made holes in fabric, so I'd have to get my shirt fixed) and held my arm up. "Hey, it's me."

They all stared. Still woozy, Target Four said, "It's a slitting SecUnit, you pussers, how stupid are you?"

Yeah, these Targets are going to be fun to chat with, I can tell already. I told him, "You're the one who got yourself bodyslammed into station detention, so let's talk about how dumb you are."

Target Four seemed shocked. "SecUnits aren't supposed to talk back," Target Five said weakly.

Tell me about it. "Cargo ship crews aren't supposed to take Port Authority supervisors as hostages, but here we all are."

From the front of the group, Aylen snapped, "Get them inside!"

The officers hurriedly milled into a more efficient configuration for taking the Targets in through the foyer. As I was rolling my sleeve down, Aylen stepped over to me. I don't know what I was expecting; nothing good, basically. But keeping her voice low, she said, "I've just had a preliminary report from the Port Authority inspectors. They did an initial scan of the *Lalow*'s storage, and the cargo containers are empty. And there's no record of anything leaving that ship."

Empty? What the fuck? I actually locked up for a second, still rolling down my sleeve. Threat assessment had just spiked and even risk assessment (which really needed to be purged and reloaded) tried to deliver a report.

I was thinking a lot of different things but the one that came out was, "So what was the transport waiting for?" I knew from my drone search that the transport Lutran had been killed in didn't have a cargo module attached. At the time, this hadn't seemed a big deal, since if the transport was sitting in dock it was probably waiting for modules to be loaded.

"A good question," Aylen said. Her expression was still in the neutral range but I could tell she was intrigued by the report, just like my threat assessment module.

I wasn't sure why she had told me this. Unless it was because she had just gotten the news and after the weapons scan fuck-up I was the only one involved with the investigation who she wasn't currently pissed off at. It would be nice if she had recognized me as the only other one here who actually knew how to investigate a suspicious incident that wasn't a cargo safety violation, but I doubted that. I said, "They know a lot about SecUnits for a ship with a non-corporate registry. We're usually only deployed as rentals on mining or other isolated contract labor installations, or by licensed security companies. They could have seen SecUnits in the media, but . . ." I couldn't finish that sentence. The fear and hatred had felt different from the fear and hatred generated by shows like *Valorous Defenders,* which sometimes featured rogue SecUnits as scary villains. The crew's reaction had felt like there was personal experience behind it, but I had no data to back that up.

"Hmm." Aylen lifted her brows. "According to their

ship's circuit report, they've never even visited a corporate dock."

"There could be an explanation," I said, because there could be, and I'm used to having to be as accurate as possible or get my neural tissue fried and old habits, etc.

"Let's ask them," she said, and went on into the station.

There was a delay, because there was documentation on the arrests that needed to be completed and the Targets all needed medical checks because that was a regulation and blah blah blah. Also more relevantly, a tech team was searching the ship for anything that looked like 1) a contact DNA cleaner and 2) something that could cause the visual jamming effect with the transit ring's surveillance camera or 3) a suspiciously fluid-stained floater cart. It also gave the Port Authority more time to pull corroborating documentation about the ship and the missing/nonexistent cargo.

I had feed messages; one from Ratthi asking if everything was okay and had I caught the murderer yet, one from Gurathin which was the same except he didn't ask if I was okay, and one from Pin-Lee saying she wanted me to contact her now, no she meant right now, it was important.

I had followed the others into the main office space on

level two, which had a large holo map of the whole station in the center, with a running status display on all station locks, air walls, and other safety systems, plus a scroll of data on cargo regulation checks throughout the port. It was surrounded by work areas and floating display surfaces. Also way too many containers with food residue, ugh. Several humans were sitting around working in their feeds and none of them looked up when I came in.

I found an unoccupied corner to stand in and sent acknowledgments/reply-laters to Ratthi and Gurathin, and tapped Pin-Lee's feed.

The first thing she sent was *I saw the update Indah sent to Mensah about an incident in the cargo dock. Is it GrayCris?*

I told her, *I don't know.* I just didn't have enough data yet for my percentages to be meaningful as anything other than theoretical shit-talking, even with the info Aylen had given me. I added, *It might be.*

Her feed voice sounded weary. *Are we ever going to be at a point where we can forget about those assholes?*

I didn't want to just say "eventually" so I told her, *I can't give you a timeline. But GrayCris can't get the currency to buy the company off, and even if they could, it's too late for that.* GrayCris had ordered a security firm to attack a company gunship, and worse, almost succeeded. There was no going back from that, at least as far as the company was concerned.

Farid came into the room, spotted me, and came over to say, "Uh, we're making tea. Do you—"

I paused my feed and told him, "I don't eat."

"Oh, right." He wandered off.

Pin-Lee sent, *There's been a Station Security request for documents from the General Counsel's office relating to cargo brokering between the Corporation Rim and outsystem polities and trading concerns. It sounds like they're looking at a possible fraud or smuggling investigation to go along with the murder. Do you want a copy of the report when we send it?*

Yes. Farid was back, this time waving at me to follow him. *I have to go.*

Find out what the hell is going on, Pin-Lee sent back, and cut the connection.

I followed Farid out of the work space and around into a conference room. Indah and Tural were seated at a table facing a large floating display. It was divided into three separate sections, each showing a different much smaller conference room. In each room was a response team officer, sitting across from a Target. Aylen was in the room with Target Five (yeah, I had picked Target Five as the one who probably knew the most about whatever it was they were doing) and the other two officers were with Targets Two and Four. One and Three were probably still in Medical.

I pulled the individual feeds so I could put them into separate inputs, in case I wanted to review them later. Right now

Aylen and the other officers were explaining to their individual Targets what rights they had as detainees in Preservation Alliance territory. (It was a lot of rights. I was pretty sure it was more rights than a human who hadn't been detained by Station Security had in the Corporation Rim.)

Chairs were scattered around and Indah waved me toward one, so I sat down. Again, it was a little, more than a little, weird. I was in a Station Security office, sitting down. (Non-rogue SecUnits aren't allowed to sit down on duty, or off duty, if there's any chance of being caught.)

Farid, Tifany, and three other officers stood back in the doorway to watch. (I will never figure out how humans decide who gets to sit where and do what, it's never the same.) (There were more cups and small plates with food residue on the table. They're always eating.)

On the three feeds, Aylen and the other two officers started the initial questions, basically "who are you," "why are you here on Preservation Station," and "what the hell were you thinking?"

The Targets' stories were fairly consistent: they were traders originating in what they called an indie station designated WayBrogatan (a quick search on the Preservation public library feed confirmed its existence) and they shipped small cargos on a regular route that never, ever, at any point intersected the Corporation Rim. And they never took on passengers, no, no way no how, never! Way-

Brogatan had special regulations and they weren't licensed for it. (That was Target Five's earnest contribution.)

Tural muttered, "Because crews who take station staff hostage are going to be sticklers for licensing regulations."

Indah agreed. "Whatever they're afraid of, it's about passengers and cargo." She tapped the investigators' private feed, which I had not been given access to and did not hack, because apparently I get to sit in a chair but not participate.

The other two officers, Soire with Target Two and Matif with Target Four, started in with questions about the ship's cargo definitely-not-passenger route, making the Targets go over what the ship had been carrying and what it had dropped off and picked up in exhaustive detail.

Aylen worked on that with Target Five, then smiled, not in a friendly way, and said, "Now. Care to explain why you tried to abduct a Station Security officer and the Port Authority supervisor?"

"Too soon?" Farid asked Indah.

She shook her head slightly. "Maybe not."

Target Five vibrated with dismay. "I didn't—We didn't do that—It was a misunderstanding—"

Weirdly, I got the sense that was true. It had been a misunderstanding.

Aylen said, "Before you argue with me about it, please recall that I was the Station Security officer you abducted."

"But—It was—" Target Five subsided and looked glum.

"Attempted abduction is the charge my senior is at this moment bringing to the Preservation Station judge-advocate." Since Aylen's senior was at this moment sitting with her arms folded intently watching the display, I guess this was a tactic. It seemed really transparent to me, but then I wasn't the one who'd landed myself in detention for what I was beginning to think was not monumental stupidity, but just a monumentally stupid mistake.

Aylen listened to Target Five sputter and protest. She said finally, "Unless you have an explanation?"

"We're just shipping cargo," Target Five said, too desperately. "It was a mistake. We overreacted. Fenn and Miro would never hurt anybody."

"It didn't look that way from the other side of the guns they had aimed at my face." Aylen was still calm and pointed.

I said, "They were expecting someone else. Someone they didn't know. They thought Aylen was lying about being Station Security."

All the humans in the room turned to look at me. I always hate that, but Tifany was nodding, and Indah said, "I'm leaning that way myself."

Targets Two and Four had been giving very convincing descriptions of their cargo route. Clearly they had taken some effort to get their stories straight. But Target Four had gotten the too-detailed story confused after the third stop and was now winging it very badly. It could have just been that Target Four had a bad memory. (I was always having to remember that humans didn't have full access to the archives stored in their neural tissue, which explained a lot about their behavior.)

Indah was subvocalizing on her feed. Aylen paused to listen, then said, "Who did you think we were?"

Target Five flustered, then leaned forward, confiding now. "The rings we go to aren't nice like this one, you can get your ship raided by the people who work there. That's what we thought it was."

Aylen nodded, like there was some tiny chance in the realm of possibility that she was buying that. "These rings are in the Corporation Rim?"

"No, no, no." Target Five did an agitated shaking movement that was apparently emphatic denial. "We've never been there. Too many permits, we can't afford it. And it's dangerous."

Aylen eyed her. Then she said, "Do you recognize this person?" and used her feed to throw an image of Lutran up on the room's display surface.

The image wasn't one of the good close-ups of Dead Lutran but the one of him alive, from the hostel. Scanners had been activated in the conference room and the real-time reports were running alongside the video display. As part of the rights thing, Aylen had told Target Five the scanner would be on, which I thought was playing way too fair, but maybe not, because Target Five didn't show an elevated heart rate or any other neural cues indicating recognition.

Target Five frowned, a clearly "why the fuck is she asking me this" expression. She said, "Uh . . . No."

Matif and Soire were getting similar reactions: Target Two clearly thought it was a trick and Target Four demanded to know who "that picker" was.

The humans all looked at the scan results and I said, "Chances that they're lying are below 20 percent." I had tapped the scanner's raw feed so I could process the data faster. (Tapping a feed that's being displayed in front of me is not hacking.)

Everybody looked at me again, then at Indah, who nodded, her gaze not leaving the display of Target Five's face. It looked like she knew what she was doing. It would be interesting to compare her data to mine. Then I remembered the main reason I was doing this was to make sure there was no connection to GrayCris and I wasn't going to refine my methods, such as they were. (What they were being mostly: crap I made up on the spot as I needed it that sort of worked, and leftover company code analysis.)

Aylen tilted her head, an unconscious gesture while she was receiving feed reports from Matif and Soire. She said, "Here's a better view of his face."

This time Lutran was dead in the image, lying where he had been dumped in the corridor junction. Target Five shook her head slowly, eyes narrowing. "No. I don't know this person. Why are you asking me about them?"

Similar reactions from Targets Two and Four. (Well, Four wanted to know if it was the same person in the two images. Matif looked like someone who was desperately repressing the urge to sigh.)

From Aylen's briefly preoccupied expression, I thought Indah had delivered another instruction via the feed. Then Aylen said, "His name was Lutran. He was found—"

She stopped abruptly because the scanner spiked. Target Five had had a reaction, a controlled flinch, and her skin was flushing as her internal fluids moved around. Target Two blinked rapidly, also flushing. Four said, "Fuck no."

Indah said softly, "Oh, now, here we go."

Aylen asked Target Five, "So you do know him?"

Target Five forced her expression back to blankness. "No."

Target Two folded her arms and pushed back in her chair. "I'm finished talking. You go ahead and throw us in detent."

Target Four said worriedly, "What about the others?"

Matif's expression of borderline frustration snapped to calm and neutral, but he was probably lucky the scanner wasn't pointed at him. He said, "I'll check. Can you tell me their names? Describe them?"

Aylen and Soire both stopped to listen as Target Four described ten humans, three of them adolescents. Apparently his memory was terrible for lies but great for the truth, and I didn't (and the scanner didn't) think he was making any of it up.

Matif leaned forward, making sure his feed recording was getting all the details. "You're saying these people should be with Lutran?"

"He was taking them home, to a home." Target Four tapped the table earnestly. "We never saw him, you know, compartmentalize to make it hard for them to catch everybody."

"Them?" Matif asked. "Who is them?"

Target Four said, "The Brehars. It's Brehar something."

I ran a quick public library query while the humans were fumbling to access their interfaces. "Possibly BreharWall-Han. It's a mining corporate . . ." I pulled more results, looking for connections. Oh, there was a big one. "It owns a system only one direct twenty-eight cycle wormhole jump from WayBrogatan."

Indah's whole face was scrunched in concentration. Tural whispered, "People. The *Lalow* was smuggling people."

Soire was having Target Two taken to the holding cell, but Aylen's face had gone preoccupied as she listened to Matif's feed. Target Five watched her, frowning in growing consternation. "Miro's talking, isn't he?" she said in despair.

Indah relayed my info to Matif, who asked Target Four, "These people came from BreharWallHan?"

"Yeah, they were slaves," Target Four told him. "They call it something else, but it's slaves, right, dah? That's what it is. Out in the rocks."

Putting together Target Four's story with what my library searches were turning up, BreharWallHan had a mining operation in an asteroid belt. The type of mining meant the contract labor had the ability to move around, to go from one asteroid to another, but they had no way to get anywhere else in the system, or out of it, and BreharWallHan controlled all access to supplies. But someone (Target Four either wouldn't or couldn't supply a name) had started an operation where contract laborers would make their way to the edge of the asteroid field, where a ship would slip in, pick them up, and take them away via the wormhole, to a point where the Targets aboard the *Lalow* would meet them and take them to a station where they would find the next step in their escape route.

"The corporates don't notice?" Matif was fascinated but skeptical. "You taking out so many people at one time?"

Target Four was unfazed. "Cause we're taking out their kids, dah. These people been out in those rocks so long they got kids older than me."

Behind me, Tifany said, "What the fuck?"

"Wait, wait." Matif was having a moment. "Are you

saying these people were shipped to this belt as contract labor, but they've been there so long they've had families—children—and those children are being born into slavery? They aren't allowed to leave?"

"I know." Target Four spread his big hands on the table. "Penis move, right? That's why we're doing this, dah. Our grandperson was contract labor, like back in the back of time, before they got away and bought the ship."

Aylen told Target Five, "Oh yes, he's telling us everything."

Target Five tried, "He has a head injury."

Aylen was unimpressed. "He seems perfectly lucid." Indah was subvocalizing again, talking to Aylen on her feed. "Even if you took payment to bring those people here, it's not illegal, and it's not illegal to be a contract labor refugee on Preservation. You can tell us where they are, we'll get them proper help. But you need to tell us how Lutran fits in to this."

Matif had just said, "But what did this have to do with Lutran?"

"He was the one, the plan person, right?" Target Four said. "He was supposed to handle what happened next."

"What happened next?" Matif asked.

Target Four put his hands in the air. "I don't know, that's what I was asking you."

Target Five slumped back in her chair, telling Aylen,

"Lutran was our contact, he always meets us at the station, whichever one it is." She added miserably, "If somebody killed him, they know about us."

I said, "The perpetrator is a BreharWallHan agent." I mean, probably. The chances were running over 85 percent.

Indah flicked her fingers at the display surfaces, and Aylen and Matif stopped talking. She said, "Not necessarily. We need to find out what happened aboard that transport. We know Lutran used it to get here, that it was involved in a cargo transfer contract with the *Lalow*, and that Lutran was killed aboard it. What does that tell us?"

Tural said, "I bet the refugees were meant to go aboard the transport, to be taken to its next destination." They made a vague gesture. "The refugees either never made it to the transport, or they were killed as well, and . . . we just haven't found their bodies yet."

Indah was frowning. "Or the refugees killed Lutran? Because he demanded something from them, like payment?"

I said, "What did the review of the Merchant Docks surveillance video show?"

Yeah, it was a trick question. I knew from my drones still out in the main office area that the video had just been transferred from PortAuthSys to StationSecSys, and none of the humans working on the case had had a chance to download the files yet.

Indah looked at me, and I realized that she knew exactly what I was doing. She said, "If that's your way of asking if you can review the video, then yes." She nodded to Tural.

On reflection, I could have handled that better.

Tural got into their feed and gave my feed ID permission to download the video. I pulled the files while they were explaining how to access and play the material, and got to work.

Indah signaled for the questioning to continue, but there wasn't much left to find out. Target Five gave in and supported Target Four's version of the story, and they both insisted that they didn't know what was supposed to happen after the refugees disembarked. All they knew was that Lutran would take care of getting them off the station to safety.

We needed to find out where the refugees were now, if they were either a) murderees or b) murderers. Concentrating on the video taken in the area around the *Lalow*'s dock, within 1.3 minutes I had isolated the moments when the refugees had left the ship. That gave us more to work with than just the descriptions Target Five had provided to Matif, though the camera's estimates weren't as good as full body scans.

The refugees were dressed in work clothes, and a few had small shoulder bags. They looked lost, stopping to check the feed markers frequently and moving slowly, as if they had never seen a station like this before. (Trapped in a contract labor camp spread out over an asteroid field, they probably hadn't.) It didn't catch any attention in this section of the docks, where ships from a wide range of places disembarked a lot of humans who had no clue what they were doing. And one of the regular-route merchants had just set a large noisy crew loose, plus there were three cargos being unloaded with varying degrees of efficiency and confusion. The *Lalow* had probably waited until the docks had gotten busy, to let the refugees mix with the crowd. The Port Authority personnel were obviously too worried about humans causing hauler bot accidents to notice the quiet group hesitantly crossing the embarkation floor.

I spotted Lutran entering the Merchant Docks one minute after the refugees left the *Lalow*. Seventeen minutes later, he left again. He had managed to avoid any cameras while inside the docks, so there was no indication of what he had done while there. It was too bad he was dead; for a human, he had been pretty good at this.

I sent the images of the refugees to Indah and Tural, then checked the video near the Merchant Dock exits to see if we could get some idea of where the refugees had headed next.

Then it got weird.

It got so weird I took extra time running the video back and forth, checking for anomalies and edits.

The Targets had been sent to detention cells to wait, and Aylen, Matif, and Soire had joined Indah and Tural to make exclamations over what they had found out instead of anything more useful. I said, "They never left the Merchant Docks."

"What?" Indah turned toward me.

I threw the video onto one of the display surfaces. I accelerated the speed, pausing it for two seconds when any human, augmented human, or bot left either of the two exits. "There's no sign of any member of the refugee party leaving the Merchant Docks. They disappear somewhere between the dockside cameras and the exit cameras' fields of view."

The humans stared at the video, Aylen moving so she could see better. "They've changed their appearances—" Soire began.

"Body types don't match." Since the security cameras used the same calibration standards, it had been easy to include a comparison check in the search. The security system noted feed IDs of known humans and augmented humans (Security officers, Port Authority staff, the merchant crews who did regular runs to Preservation) and I'd used them to annotate my sped-up video. There were only seven unidentified humans who had wandered out of the dock exits during our time frame, none matching the body type estimates the system had taken from the refugees, and all seven unidentified humans had returned via the dock entrance. I matched them on the dockside camera returning to their ships.

Aylen shook her head and reached for a jacket slung over a chair. She had the expression of someone who wanted to curse a lot but wasn't going to. "We need to get over there and find them."

Because obviously, if they hadn't left, they were still there.

Whatever, the chance that it was GrayCris activity that had caused Lutran's death was dropping rapidly. I could leave Station Security to finish up. Go back and catch up on my media while I kept watch over Mensah. I should do that. The rest of this was Station Security's job, I could leave. I could pretend to be the enigmatic SecUnit and just get up and walk out. Pin-Lee had written my employment contract that way, so I could just leave.

I wasn't leaving.

I didn't think I'd have a better time to push for this. I waited until Indah finished ordering all response teams into the Merchant Docks for a search, then said, "Has there been a diagnostic analysis of StationSec and PortAuth and all associated systems?"

Aylen, Matif, and Soire were already on the way out to get their gear and Tural was in the feed mobilizing the tech crew. Aylen stopped but Indah waved her on to keep moving.

As the door slid shut behind them, Indah said impatiently, "No, not since you asked the first time and I told you the analysts had checked for hacks and there was nothing, no alerts had been tripped."

Alerts? She hadn't said that the first time. "They relied on alerts?"

Tural was listening now, their face turned guarded in that very familiar "someone else is getting in trouble" way. Indah said flatly, "I don't know. The report they sent said that in their opinion, there had been no hack."

I said, "With the safety of the station depending on it, are you sure you don't want a second opinion?"

There was a moment, slightly fraught. Indah said, "You want access to our systems."

I could go into all my reasoning and my threat assessment module's indicator that there was only a 35 percent chance there was a jamming device present on this station. (I was 86 percent certain that type of device actually existed somewhere, but I just didn't think it would be easily available, even to a security company. Mainly because, if something like that was easy to obtain, the company would have countermeasures for its SecSystems, and I would know about it. Obviously, it could have been a casualty of one of my memory wipes, or it could be something only available outside the Corporation Rim, but still.) If someone had gotten far enough into the port's system to tamper with the camera video, they might have done/do anything.

I could have also said that Indah had me, the best resource Station Security could have for this situation, and she was too afraid to use me. I said, "To check for hacking, yes."

Tural shifted uneasily, but they were brave, and said, "We should make sure. If there has been interference with our camera video, we could be looking for the refugees in the wrong place."

Indah didn't reply. It occurred to me if she turned me down, I was going to feel . . . something, probably general humiliation, and basically like an idiot. Which sucked, because I had set myself up yet again. But what she said was, "How much access would you need? And how long would it take?"

Okay, huh. "Admin access, under five minutes." I know, five minutes was a hilariously long time, but I wanted a good long look around while I was in there.

Indah didn't reply. I figured it was about 40/60 between "it will take over the station and kill us all" and "this isn't the worst idea I ever heard." Then she said, "Only five minutes?"

"I'm fast," I said. "If the dock surveillance system is hacked, then everything on the Port Authority systems could be compromised."

Indah said, "You don't have to spell it out quite so pointedly, I understand the consequences. But we have data protection on the security systems—"

Data protection, right. Guess what provides your data protection—another security system. I had to make her understand. "And that's what everybody says. When I walked onto TranRollinHyfa and walked out with Dr. Mensah, that's exactly what they said."

(I know, very dramatic and also inaccurate. Dr. Mensah walked out barefoot and I limped out leaning on Ratthi and Gurathin. But you see my point.)

Indah's mouth twisted in skepticism. Okay, fine then. I said, "Are the systems in the Security Station offices monitored for breach attempts?"

Her brow furrowed. "Yes."

I'd chosen the StationSec office because it had a nested set of high security systems not connected to the Port Authority, so a demonstration there was unlikely to alert our hostile. I had several options to go with, having been in the systems and rummaged around a little when Mensah had first brought me here, before I stupidly promised not to touch anything. I decided on something showy.

I took control of the visual and audio displays in the main work space. Through the open door, we heard the humans in there make startled noises. Indah glared at me. "What did you—"

I put a camera view up on a display surface. In the main office area, the three-dimensional station safety map was now showing episode 256 of *The Rise and Fall of Sanctuary Moon,* the scene 32.3 minutes in when the solicitor, her bodyguard, and the personnel supervisor are having a relationship argument that is abruptly cut off when a raider ship crashes into the shuttle bay.

Tifany, Aylen, and the others getting ready for the search stared at it in bafflement. "What the balls?" somebody said.

Indah's face was . . . interesting. She gestured to the display surface. "How are you getting this view of the room? There's no camera in there."

I could have used a drone's camera, but this way made for a better demonstration. "It's Farid's vest cam," I told her.

Indah grimaced. "You've made your point. Fix the screen," she said. "And check the systems for hacking."

Chapter Six

AFTER ALL THAT, IT took me six minutes to find out the dock surveillance system had not been hacked.

I didn't find anything. No aberrations in the logs, no anomalous deletions, no foreign code, no traces at all.

So, that's just great.

There had to be something I was missing. Or maybe I'm just a robot with enough human neural tissue jammed in my head to make me stupid who should have stayed with the company, guarding contract labor and staring at walls.

Fortunately Indah and Tural had followed the others out to the main office to get their gear for the search, and I could have an emotion on my face in relative private.

I'd decided to stay, but I really wanted to leave.

I'd been so sure I was right.

I went out into the main office and told Indah, "There's no hack. The surveillance system was clear."

I was braced for something, I had no idea what. But the fleeting look of disappointment that crossed Indah's face wasn't it. She grimaced, and used the feed to revoke my system access.

Aylen came in from the other room, pulling on a deflection vest. "The off shift volunteered to come in early," she said. "And Supervisor Gamila is helping with coordination."

"Good, take all of them." Indah glanced at me. "And SecUnit."

Well, fine.

An evidence team was still searching the *Lalow* and Indah sent them an order via the feed that they might be looking for "signs of body disposal." One theory was that the refugees had been killed in the docks by the *Lalow*'s crew and the remains somehow smuggled back into their ship.

(I know, if they could do that to ten refugees why didn't they do that to Lutran? But sometimes you have to look into every possibility, even the dumb ones.)

The *Lalow* search team had already found evidence that the refugees really had been aboard long enough to get here from a point near the BreharWallHan mining field: the ship's recycler stats showed waste and water conversion from at least fifteen humans for the duration of the trip, and the ship's stores had a suspiciously large amount of bedding and food, plus games for pre-adolescents.

(Yes, again, I know. Why bring them all the way here

alive and in relative comfort, let them disembark, then kill them? Theoretically the *Lalow* crew could have been paid to do that, but if there had been a hard currency transfer it wouldn't have occurred on station so there was no way we could find that out.)

Station Security was only allowed to keep the *Lalow* for one Preservation day-cycle before they either had to charge the crew with something or let them go. Indah could charge them with the threatening and imprisoning or whatever else they had done to Aylen and Supervisor Gamila any-time she wanted to give us more time to investigate, but she was holding off. Before we had left for the Merchant Docks again, Indah told the special investigation team, "If this cir-cus act is telling the truth and they're the only lifeline those people trapped at BreharWallHan have, then we'll release them without charge. Until then I don't want to risk any information about any of this getting into outsystem news-feeds. Normally this isn't a problem but—" She pointed her eyebrows at me. "We seem to be getting a lot of attention from the Corporation Rim lately."

Like that's my fault.

She continued, "I think we all realize by now that be-tween the murder and the missing individuals, this is un-likely to be a single local actor. Our most likely perpetrators will be agents of the corporate entity BreharWallHan, who came here specifically to stop this refugee operation. With the port closed, they're trapped here."

I was with her right up until the "they're trapped here" part. I wasn't willing to count on that because it involved depending on humans and bots and systems I didn't have access to.

Aylen had formed up two more teams to search the ships in dock, though Station Security was starting to run short of personnel. There were ships not attached to the docks, in holding positions around the station, who had either been stopped in the middle of approach or departure by the closure of the port. If we didn't find anything in the port, the ships stopped in departure were going to have to be searched next. Even with the responder patrolling out there to keep everybody from leaving, that was going to be a mess.

From what I could hear over the team feed channel, the ships in dock were cooperating with the search so far. The teams were going with the story that they were looking for "adults and adolescents who might be in the company of individuals who had committed violent acts on station," which was probably true.

No, I was not helping with the ship-to-ship search because the humans thought there would be "panic and resistance" if any of the search teams tried to board with a

SecUnit. (Yeah, let's revisit that the next time you get held hostage.)

So I was searching the dock utility areas with the hazardous materials safety techs and the cargo bots. The modules had drives but they weren't the kind you could turn on inside the station, so the cargo bots lifted and moved them for us so the techs could check the interiors.

Since this was the oldest part of the transit ring, we were moving along the stationside of the dock area, climbing in and out of outdated cargo storage chambers, safety equipment deployment corrals, office spaces that were long abandoned to storage. One of the techs muttered, "We can take our video and make a historical documentary."

Another tech walked up to me. "Um, SecUnit, we need someone to help move this cabinet—"

"Then you should find someone to do that for you." I was not in the mood.

"Well, it's in a small space and JollyBaby can't fit." They gestured to the cargo bot looming over us.

"Its name is not JollyBaby." Tell me its name is not Jolly-Baby. It was five meters tall sitting in a crouch and looked like the mobile version of something you used to dig mining shafts.

JollyBaby broadcast to the feed: *ID=JollyBaby*. The other cargo bots and everything in the bay with a processing capability larger than a drone all immediately pinged it back, and added amusement sigils, like it was a stupid private joke.

I said, "You have to be shitting me." I already wanted to walk out an airlock and this didn't help. (The only thing worse than humans infantilizing bots was bots infantilizing themselves.)

JollyBaby secured a private connection with me and sent: *Re: previous message=joke.* And it added its actual ID, which was its hard feed address. So it was a stupid private joke. I don't think that made it any better.

The human was still looking at me helplessly and I said, "Where the fuck is the Port Authority bot? Isn't this its job?" All those arms had to be good for something besides holding hatches open.

The human shrugged vaguely. "I think it's with the Port Authority supervisor. It doesn't work in these docks." Jolly-Baby sent me another private message: *Balin not equal cargo hauler Balin equal cargo management.*

Balin didn't lift heavy things? Well, fuck Balin then. I said, "All right, where's the fucking cabinet?"

On the team channel, Matif was saying to Indah, *But would these refugees have a device that let them jam the port cameras?* He didn't think the refugees were responsible for killing Lutran, either. He added, *And know they could call a cart to the transport to dump the body? That seems like it has to be someone who was already here on station.*

The other conversation was Tural and Aylen, with Tural saying, *Why didn't the refugees just stop here? Why take the transport somewhere else?*

Aylen replied, *Maybe another group, or groups did. But they couldn't bring all the groups here without the risk that someone would find out about the scheme and expose it.*

No shuttles had left for the planet or any other insystem destination in the incident time frame, and I guess we were all just assuming the refugees hadn't been spaced, though the exterior station scan results hadn't come back yet.

The refugees couldn't have gotten off this dock, and Lutran's killer couldn't have entered his transport without the cameras' data on the PA systems being hacked. And I had of course proved that it hadn't.

Which . . . was a massive fuck-up on my part.

Because this was the kind of hacking a SecUnit could do, specifically a CombatUnit. If this was a BreharWallHan operation to stop the escapes, they might have brought in a security company with a CombatUnit doing exactly the kind of thing I had pretended to do on Milu: operating almost independently with a human supervisor planted somewhere on station. I just hadn't been good enough to find that Unit's trail in the PA's system.

I didn't know what I was going to do. I could call Mensah and ask for advice, which would actually be a cover for asking her to fix my fuck-up. Except I had no evidence of the hack; I couldn't even prove it to myself, so I didn't know how Mensah could fix it.

On the comm, one of the techs said, "Officer Aylen." It was the one who had made the comment about a historical documentary on the crap stored in the private docks. "I've got a problem with the empty modules."

Sounding frustrated, Aylen answered, "What problem?"

The tech explained, "According to the inventory, we're missing one. I'm guessing it's outside for transfer, so we need it brought in so we can verify—"

I cut into the channel and said, "A module is missing?" at the same time as Indah, Aylen, and Soire. Matif was already on the feed telling the Port Authority that we needed the spare-module use records and could they confirm an empty module outside the station?

"Ask them who authorized that transfer," Soire told Matif at the same time Aylen said, "Those modules can be pressurized, correct?"

I said, "Correct." I was already walking out of the ancient storage compartment back toward the embarkation area. They could finish the historical documentary without my help. If I was going to be useless, I could at least be useless where stuff was going on.

Indah said, "Find that fucking module."

I reached what the humans were calling the "mobile

command center," which was actually just one of the portable Port Authority terminal and display surfaces for accessing all the transit ring's traffic data. Indah stood next to it with PA Supervisor Gamila. Aylen, Tural, and other officers and techs sprinted in from different directions. Gamila controlled the terminal via her feed, the display surface floating above her head and flicking through sensor views of the outside hull of the station. I picked up a live feed from the station responder on picket duty, supplying alternate sensor views. Gamila was talking to someone on the responder, saying, "No, those modules are for the *Walks Silent Shores,* that's a scheduled transfer, they're all accounted for. We're looking for a single unregistered module—"

No authorized transfer, Matif reported via the Station Security feed. *It's just missing.*

Soire added, *Somebody must have deleted its records.*

(If it seems like they twigged to this faster than they had anything else, it was because cargo safety/smuggling and hazardous material prevention was actually most of their job. I'm sure they were great at talking down aggressively intoxicated humans, too.)

Still breathing hard from running down the dock, Aylen said to Tural, "Could someone install longterm life support in one of those things?"

"Theoretically, I guess." Tural's face scrunched with worry. "Not in a hurry. These are just transfer modules.

They're pressurized and they hold air, but . . . They're not meant for . . ."

They're not meant for anything that needs to breathe, not for longer than a cycle or so, Tural meant. If the refugees were in there, they didn't have much time left.

As a means to quickly move humans from the private Merchant Docks to a transport, it would have been fine, especially on a small transit ring like this one where the trip would have taken no more than half an hour at most. It was the ideal means of getting them from one end of the station to the other with no one noticing, especially if you were desperate to cover your tracks and throw off any corporate pursuit.

"Was this a trick all along?" Tifany said, low-voiced. She and Farid were standing next to me, for some reason. "Bring those people here, then put them on the module to kill them?"

"No, that's way too elaborate, if they just want to murder whoever tries to escape," Farid told her.

Well, yeah. The *Lalow* had thought it was delivering the group of refugees to the next step in their route to safety. The crew had sent the refugees out to meet their contact, who they knew was called Lutran, though they didn't know what he looked like. There had been no reported disruptions on the embarkation floor, no fight, no struggle picked up by the cameras, so the refugees had had no idea they were in danger.

So, working theory: Lutran meets the refugees and gets them to board the module that is due to be transferred from the Merchant Docks to his transport waiting in the Public Docks. (The transfers were all done by bot; haulers moved the recently loaded modules to the lock and pushed them out. If it was an inert module, the cargo bots would take it and attach it to its transport. If it was a powered module, the cargo bots would place it on one of the set paths around the station where it would get a go-signal and then head toward its destination. When it arrived, another cargo bot, or the transport itself if it had the right configuration, would attach the module.) With the refugees safe aboard the module, Lutran then goes back to his transport to make sure the module attaches correctly when it arrives and that the refugees get aboard. But it's not there, the module has been diverted to an unknown destination. Someone else is aboard the transport, and that person kills Lutran. Then that person, who somehow has hacked the PA's systems, deletes the record of Lutran's module transfer.

This scenario was the most likely one, the probability was 86 percent, easily. But it was impossible unless the perpetrator could 1) hack Lutran's transport, 2) hack the PortAuth surveillance cameras, and 3) hack the PortAuth transfer records.

So where was the module? It couldn't just be floating around out there. The responder would have found it by now. Wherever it had gone, it must have looked like it was headed toward a legitimate destination, so the systems that did nothing but scan and monitor all station traffic wouldn't alert on it.

It had to be attached to a ship.

And that ship, and the BreharWallHan agents, was still out there. It had been unable to leave before Lutran was discovered and the port closed. Most stations wouldn't close their transit rings because someone found a dead body, but most stations weren't as short on random dead bodies as this one.

The BreharWallHan ship hadn't run, or tried to fight the responder, because Indah was right, they wanted to keep it quiet. They wanted the *Lalow* to continue its part of the operation until the BreharWallHan agents could trace all the routes, all the stations where refugees had been transferred, maybe until they could figure out where the pick-up point was inside the mining field.

All of this was leading to the conclusion . . . Oh, shit.

Which meant . . . I had to stop the search.

I could call Mensah and get her to make Indah listen to me. I could do that, but I still thought it would sound a lot like the time Mensah's youngest child had got hold of the comm and demanded that Mensah tell an older sibling to stop taking all the squash dumplings. Mensah could make Indah listen to me, but it would waste time, and Indah being made to listen to me against her will was step one of a failure scenario. (I don't know much about human interactions, but even I knew that.) I had to get Indah to trust me.

I could start by talking to her, I guess, I had actually not tried that yet, really.

I secured a protected feed connection with her and sent, *Senior Officer Indah, you have to stop the search. The module must be attached to a ship still holding position off the station. If the BreharWallHan agents know we've found the module, they'll kill the refugees and run. Everything on the Port Authority systems has to be treated as compromised. Whoever is on that ship could be using the dock cameras and Supervisor Gamila's comm to listen to you and your officers right now. If you find the module while they're listening—*

She objected, *You said that system wasn't hacked.*

I said, *I'm wrong. Whoever did this is good enough not to leave any indication they were in the system. They are as good at this or better than I am.* (Oh yeah, it hurt to say that.)

Aylen was trying to say something to her and Indah held up a hand to show she was on her feed. Her eyes were narrow and her mouth was thin. I had no idea what that meant. She said, *How do you know this hacker isn't listening to you right now?*

Because that's how fuckers get permanently deleted, is what I wanted to say. What I actually said was, *I can secure my own internal system. I can't secure the Port Authority's systems or yours.*

Indah hesitated, then switched to her all-team comm, "Aylen, come with me, we've got to reorganize this. I think we're wrong about that module." She told Matif, "Tell the search parties to resume, and we're extending the search to the Public Docks."

Matif glanced at Soire, clearly dubious. "Uh, all right. I mean, yes, Senior."

Indah and Aylen were already walking away and I followed them. Keeping her voice low, Indah said, "Comms off." Aylen immediately complied and my drone video showed a visible shift in her attitude, from confused protest to still confused but no longer protesting.

Indah added, "SecUnit, I assume you can get me a secure connection to the station responder?"

"Yes. This way." I secured a connection with Dr. Mensah's feed. *Hi. I have a request.*

I knew from her guard drones that she was still in the council offices on the other side of the station mall, working in her feed. *What's up?*

Senior Indah and I need to borrow your private office.

Mensah's private office was close by, in the admin block with the Port Authority. But the important part was that her comm and security monitoring wasn't connected to either StationSec or any of the PortAuth systems, it was a separate secure system used by the council.

And it was really secure, because one of the first jobs Mensah had got for me was to make sure it was "up to date and resistant to corporate or other incursion."

It was such a relief to step into a place where I had control of the security. As we crossed the tiled floor of the lobby I felt the tension in the organic parts of my back ease. Mensah had notified her staff to let us through, and I removed us from the surveillance camera, just in case.

One of her assistants opened the inner office for us. He had already closed and opaqued the transparent doors on the balcony that looked out over the admin plaza. He was used to me and used to confidential council stuff, so he didn't even glance up at my drones, just nodded to us and slipped out as we stepped in. He said, "I'll be in the reception area, just message me when you're finished," and engaged the privacy seal on the door.

Indah had been here before but Aylen clearly hadn't, and looked around at the family images and the plants. (It was a nice office, I had spent a lot of time on the couch.) I used the feed to open the secure terminal, and the big display surface formed in the air above the desk. I opened the secure channel for Indah and for Mensah, who had been holding on her secure feed in the council offices. Then I sent a hail for the responder. When it answered, I opened the connection.

Indah ordered the responder to scan the ships in holding positions off the station and sent the module's specifications. She told them there was a possibility the Port Authority systems had been compromised and they needed to communicate only with her or Aylen, and via the council system and not Station Security's system. The responder asked for a confirmation order from the council and Mensah supplied it. Mensah then signed off, telling Indah to contact her immediately if she needed any other assistance, and Indah thanked her.

Then me, Aylen, and Indah were standing in the office looking at each other. Or they were looking at me and my drones were looking at them.

"You really think our systems are compromised?" Aylen asked.

Indah had her arms folded, her expression grim. It had occurred to me she was maybe worried about feeling stupid too, if we were wrong about this. She said, "Yes. It's the only thing that makes sense."

I had control of all inputs to this room's comm and feed, and I caught and bounced a comm call for Indah with Balin the Port Authority bot's feed ID. It was probably an important call from Gamila but if something had blown up the council's system would notify us and everything else could wait five minutes. It was time to be honest. I told Indah, "You were wrong when you said it was unlikely to be a local actor. But I think you know that now."

Indah glared at me, but it was more wry than angry. "Is that what you think? Because you keep insisting it's a mysterious ultra-hacker."

Okay, that one stung. "I didn't use the words 'mysterious' or 'ultra.'"

Aylen watched like it was one of those human games where they threw balls at each other. (I'd had to stop a lot of those while on company contracts; they violated the company personal injury safety bonds.) (Yeah, it was super fun telling the humans they couldn't do it because SecUnits always like giving their clients more reasons to hate them.) But Aylen also looked relieved. Like she was beginning to wonder if we were stupid or what. She muttered, "Thank the divine, can we talk about it like adults now?"

Indah pointed the glare at her. "If the Port Authority systems weren't hacked, then the files and camera data were altered by someone on station who has legitimate access, who knew how to cover their tracks." She made an impatient gesture. "It even fits with the tool that was used to remove contact DNA from the body. The PA uses sterilizers for hazardous material safety, they're all over the port offices."

Aylen nodded. "But who? Everyone's worked here for years, grew up here."

I told Indah, "You thought it was me."

She snorted in exasperation. "We thought it was you when we thought Lutran was a GrayCris agent. But we disproved that—I forget how many hours ago that was, this has been a long damn day."

Aylen was annoyed. "If it was you, why would you tell us where the original crime scene was, which led to finding the *Lalow* and the refugees?"

Indah added, "You are the most paranoid person I've ever met, and I've worked in criminal reform for twenty-six years."

I don't even know how to react to that. She's not wrong but hey, I need my paranoia. Speaking of which, I asked Aylen, "Where were you when Lutran was killed?"

She didn't blink. "I was on a shuttle, coming back from an assignment in FirstLanding."

"She was docking when the body was found." Indah huffed impatiently. "Give me a little credit."

The responder had kept its channel open and we could hear the crew talking in the background. "SatAmratEye5 is in the best position . . . That one's clear . . . If they aren't local they probably don't know our satellite placement . . . There we go. Senior Indah, we've got it. There's a ship with a module attached hiding in station section zero, in the shadow of the Pressy's upper hull." They were sending data and I transferred it to the big display above our heads.

It was a sensor schematic of a long shot view of the station, the curve of the ring tucked below the main structure and the shape of the giant colony ship it had been built out from. The view turned into a scan schematic and focused in on a shape huddled not far from the colony ship's starboard hull.

It wasn't a modular transport, it was a ship more like the *Lalow*. A bulky tube with round parts sticking out, and the module clamped onto its hull stood out in the sensor view like a . . . like a weird thing that shouldn't be there. Aylen swore in relief and Indah told the responder to hold position and wait for orders.

Indah said, "The priority right now is to get to those people and if they're alive, to get them out of there."

Aylen looked grim. "That's not going to be easy. It's close enough to the colony ship that we could reach it with a team in EVAC suits, but we can't arrange that from here. If the BreharWallHan agents have someone in the Port Authority who can listen in on our comms and feed, they're going to know what we're doing."

Yeah, not we, me. I said, "This is the part that's my job."

Chapter Seven

I'D BEEN BROUGHT TO Preservation on one of their older ships, which had been refitted over and over again. This section of the colony ship had never been refitted. The corridors were dingy, the paint on the dark metal patchy where it had been rubbed off by hands and shoulders.

The colony ship hadn't just been left to rot; the humans liked it too much for that. It smelled of clean emptiness in a way human places never do. Pieces of clear protective material had been placed over the occasional drawings on the bulkheads, and on the pieces of paper stuck to them and covered with scribbled handwriting and faded print. Feed markers had been installed by Station Historical/Environment Management with translations into Preservation Standard Nomenclature. My drones picked up whispers of lost-and-found notices, messhall schedules, and the rules for games I didn't recognize.

It should have been creepy. I had been in places like this that were really creepy. But this wasn't. Maybe because I knew where the humans and augmented humans who had last used this ship had gone, that their descendants were running around all over this system, and that one of them was in my secure feed right now, demanding an update.

I'm almost there, I told Aylen. *Just give me a fucking minute.*

Indah had gone back to the mobile command center to be visible, but she wanted me to have backup. Aylen was waiting at the entrance to this section of the colony ship, making sure nobody followed me up here. If she had to call in a team for help, she was going to hold off as long as possible, to keep our local actor from knowing what we were doing until hopefully it was too late.

Aylen said, *You know, swearing during operations doesn't meet the professional conduct standards of Station Security.*

By this point I knew that was Aylen's idea of a joke. I replied, *Because Senior Indah has never told anybody to fuck off.*

You have me there.

I reached the lock corridor and sent, *I'm going offline now.*

Understood, she sent back. *Good luck.*

I understand why humans say that, but luck sucks. I found the lock and dropped the EVAC suit container on the deck to expand and unpack it.

Once I had it out, I started to pull the tab to activate it. Then I processed the instructions it was loading into the feed . . . *this emergency device alerts the Port Authority emergency notification network and the transponder will send your location to* . . . Ugh, of course the EVAC suit had a transponder, this was a stripped-down emergency version for stations, not the full ship corporate-brand EVAC suits I'd used before.

The local actor, if not the hostile ship itself, was sure to be monitoring the station's search and rescue channel. They would know someone was trying to approach surreptitiously.

I was going to have to turn the transponder off. There was no way to do that via the feed so I needed to find the physical switch. I pulled the schematic from the instructions and found the transponder was buried in the sealed drive unit.

Oh, you have to be kidding me. I'd be pissed off at the humans but I had brought this thing up here without checking. Seconds were ticking away while I wasted time. I couldn't take the drive unit apart without breaking it, I had no idea how. I didn't have the ability to disguise the signal. I could jam it, but at such close range any static leakage, any hint of activity on the otherwise silent search and rescue channel, might alert the hostile ship. It would sure as hell alert me if I was in their position. There was no time to go back for another EVAC suit or . . .

Or Murderbot, you dummy, you're on a giant spaceship that has been meticulously preserved as a historical artifact. If they still had intact lunch menus from however many years ago, the chances were good they still had the safety equipment.

Big green arrows scrawled along the bulkhead pointed me toward the nearest emergency lockers and I opened the first one. The inside was neatly packed with safety supplies, all of it tagged with explanatory labels and scrawled symbols on the containers, all of it simple and easily readable for any panicky untrained human. Except I didn't have this language loaded.

So I had to go back online for a minute. I secured a connection with Ratthi and Gurathin and said, *I need help.*

They were eating together in one of the station mall's food places; Ratthi stood up and knocked his chair over and Gurathin spilled the liquid in the cup he was lifting. Ratthi said, *SecUnit, what's wrong?*

I understood the reaction. I didn't ask for help that often. I sent them my drone video: *Which one of these things is most like an EVAC suit?*

Uh, are you up in the Pressy? Ratthi asked, baffled. *The closest thing I see to an EVAC suit in there is a life-tender. But—*

There, third shelf down, with the red tags, Gurathin added. I yanked one out of the rack and he said, *Wait, why do you need it? What are you doing?*

It's a Station Security thing, I'll tell you later, I said, and cut the connection. Now that I had the name, I used the station feed to hit the public library, where I pulled a description and operating instructions from the historical records.

The life-tender wasn't so much an EVAC suit as it was a small vehicle. It opened into a kind of diamond-shaped bag with rudimentary navigation, propulsion, and life support. According to the library record, it was designed to get several humans off one ship and onto a new one, usually because the first ship was about to have a catastrophic failure. This one also had a transponder but it was set to the colony ship's comm ID, which had been delisted as an active channel and turned into an audio monument, broadcasting historical facts and stories about the colony ship's first arrival in the system. It was unlikely the hostiles would be monitoring it and the chatty broadcasts would provide cover for my comm and the life-tender's location transmissions. The library entry also said life-tenders weren't used anymore because without their transponders, they were difficult to locate and didn't meet Preservation's current safety standards. Difficult to locate sounded good, though, like the hostile ship wouldn't know it was out there unless it specifically scanned for it, which was what I needed.

The historical story currently playing on the colony ship's comm sounded interesting, so I set one of my inputs to record it as I carried the life-tender to the airlock. Following the instructions, I pulled the tabs, set the safety to active, tossed it into the lock, and cycled it through. It was old, but its sealed storage was designed to keep equipment functioning for long periods of time, just like everything else on this ship; it was how these old colony ships worked. (You couldn't be on Preservation for more than five minutes without being forced to listen to a documentary about it.)

I just hoped all the documentaries were right.

The life-tender signaled the ship's comm that it was ready and I stepped into the airlock and let it cycle shut. I could see the life-tender on the lock's camera, where it had clamped itself around the outer hatch. Wow, that is just a bag, is what that is.

I didn't need as much air as humans did, but I needed some, and it was really cold out there, in the colony ship's shadow. This meant that if the life-tender failed it would take me longer to die so I'd have longer to feel dumb about it than a human would.

So here goes. I told my drones to get in my pockets and go dormant. Then I opened the hatch and leaned out to sort of float/fall into the tender. Okay, new problem. It's really fucking dark.

The huge hull of the colony ship blocked any light from the primary, the station, the planet, whatever, which was probably why the hostile ship had picked this spot to hide.

It's cold, it's dark, whatever was generating the air smelled terrible, I'm in a bag in space. I thought about going back for the EVAC suit, but the chance that the hostiles were scanning for transponders on the station search and rescue channel was still hitting 96 percent. If what I was doing in this stupid bag was dumb, going out here with a beacon I couldn't turn off or disguise was much more dumb.

Okay, fine, let's just get it over with.

I sealed the bag's entrance and let the ship's hatch close. The tender was controlled via a local connection to its drive and navigation, so it could still be used if, say, your ship blew up and you couldn't access its comm or feed. I had the location for the hostile ship and I fed it into the simple system, and my little bag headed off through the dark.

I carefully explored the control options, and wow, I now knew why the bag was described as "difficult to locate in a combat situation" because its power supply was so minimal it was almost nonexistent. Even my body heat was already causing condensation. I found the menu for monitoring life support, such as it was. The bag had lights but turning them on would just be stupid plus I didn't really want to see what was happening.

Then the bag bumped (it wasn't really a bump, it was more like a blorp) into something solid and stopped. I checked navigation and holy shit, we're here.

The bag's sensor system was primitive but it knew it had blorped itself up against the curving hull of a ship. I detected the ship's feed connection but it was silent. Not locked down, just quiet as whoever was aboard tried to minimize contact.

Modules didn't have an airlock, they relied on attaching to the transport or station cargo lock; I wouldn't have been able to open the module's hatch for the EVAC suit without killing everyone inside, so the plan had been to get into the hostile ship through its lock and then run around getting shot and murdering my way through whoever was aboard until I could get control. (I hadn't used those exact words during the planning process with Indah and Aylen, but we all knew what we were talking about.) But my maybe-not-so-dumb bag made its own airlock, that was the whole point of it.

If I could get the refugees out of the module and over to the colony ship's lock without the hostiles even realizing I was there, then the responder would be free to take over the hostile ship.

That plan was easier plus 100 percent less murdery. And I liked it better.

Huh. I liked it better because it wasn't a CombatUnit plan, or actually a plan that humans would come up with for CombatUnits. Sneaking the endangered humans off the ship to safety and then leaving the hostiles for someone else to deal with, that was a SecUnit plan, that was what we were really designed for, despite how the company and every other corporate used us. The point was to retrieve the clients alive and fuck everything else.

Maybe I'd been waiting too long for GrayCris to show

up and try to kill us all. I was thinking like a CombatUnit, or, for fuck's sake, like a CombatBot.

I got the bag to blorp along the hull over to where the module should be, then along its side to where scan detected the outline of the module's access hatch. Once the bag was in place, its automatic functions took over and it enlarged itself to completely cover the hatch. The bag assured me it had made a secure seal. Okay, it hadn't lied to me so far.

Now this part might be tricky. I carefully felt around in the empty feed, looking for the ship's bot pilot. Oh, there it was. It was a limited bot pilot, just there to steer and dock the ship and guide it through wormholes. It was startled to be accessed, even though I was spoofing a Port Authority ID. It's usually easy to make friends with low-level bot pilots, but this one had been coded to be adversarial, directed to operate in stealth mode, and was wary of incursion attempts. It tried to alert its onboard SecSystem, but as the old saying (which I just made up) goes, if you can ping the SecUnit, it's way too late.

I took control, disabled the SecSystem, and put the bot pilot in sleep mode. Having to keep it dormant was annoying, because it limited my ability to use the ship's functions, but it meant the hostiles wouldn't be able to fly off toward the wormhole or fire weapons at the responder or whatever else they felt like shooting at.

Next I accessed the module's hatch control. I didn't want to risk trying to use the comm or feed to check if anybody was inside, because not alerting the hostiles was the whole point of going in this way.

I checked the bag's airlock seal again, then told the module to open its access hatch.

Oh, shit, my stupid, stupid feed ID that identified me as a SecUnit. Just as the hatch slid up, I switched it to the last one in my buffer, the Kiran ID I'd used on TranRollinHyfa.

The lighted interior would have blinded me if my eyes worked that way. I meant to say something before I went inside but the bag had no grav function and the module did, so let's put it this way, my entrance was abrupt and not graceful.

The module was a big oblong container with ribbed supports and racks folded into the bulkheads and no padding anywhere, making it clear it was designed for cargo, not passengers. It was colder than the bag and the air smelled wrong. The bunch of humans inside screamed and threw themselves away from the hatch that from their perspective had apparently just opened into empty space. Then they realized I was standing there and they screamed again.

Fortunately I had a lot of experience being screamed at and stared at by terrified humans. It was never comfortable, and I couldn't let my drones deploy so I had to look at them with my actual eyes, but I was sort of used to that by now. Also, I'd spent a whole trip through a wormhole pretending to be an augmented human security consultant for humans who badly needed one, so I had coping mechanisms in place. Sort of.

I held up my hands and said, "Please calm down. I'm from Preservation Station Security and I'm here to get you to safety." They huddled at the other end of the module, still staring, but I thought that was shock and surprise. I added, "You've been abducted by whoever is aboard this ship, they were not sent by your contact Lutran."

"We know that," one of the humans said. They started to unfold from defensive positions as they realized I wasn't here to shoot them. I didn't see any signs of serious injury but from the disarray of their clothes and some visible bruises, they had been knocked around in the module at some point. I wasn't picking up any augments or interfaces. Which made sense; only the non-augmented contract labor would be able to leave BreharWallHan without being traced, and the escapees would know to leave their interfaces behind. Their captors would have confiscated any comms or interfaces the *Lalow* crew had given them. Human One continued, "They're bounty-catchers, sent by the supervisors." She pointed up.

It could have been a trick but I looked up anyway. Oh shit, the module is attached to a lock. An appallingly jury-rigged lock, way too small.

The module's other hatch, the large one meant to load and unload bulk cargo, was open, sealed directly against the hull of the ship. For fuck's sake, I could see part of the ship's registration number.

The ship's lock, roughly in the center of the opening, was only about two meters square and had no transparent panel, just a camera, and no controls to open it from this side. It was terrifying, both from a safety standpoint and an "oh shit" standpoint. It's a good thing I can have a horrified emotional reaction while also simultaneously pulling the latest video out of the ship's SecSystem, deleting myself and the open hatch, and starting a loop so if any hostiles checked their module camera, everything would look normal. Was there even an air wall behind that lock? Holy shit, who does this?

The hostiles up in the ship might have heard the screaming. I lowered my voice. "We need to get you out of here now." I hadn't meant to say that next but it just came out, because this could be such a disaster. All the hostiles had to do was disengage the seal on the module and I'd lose every one of the humans. With the bot pilot down, they couldn't disengage via the ship's feed, but the chance that the seal had a manual release was high.

My bag, blorping quietly to itself on the access hatch, was starting to look really friendly in comparison.

I connected to the hostile ship's hamstrung SecSystem

again and started to feel for more cameras. There wasn't a full set; obviously this crew didn't like the idea of a video record of all the fun they were having while hunting contract labor refugees. But I needed to get a view of the compartment on the other side of the hatch of jury-rigged terror.

"So your station can send us back to the supervisors and get the bounty?" Human One said. The humans were all shivering and showing various signs of physical and emotional distress. I didn't know what the air quality rating was in here but I could guess it wasn't good. This was no time to explain Preservation's attitude toward forced labor and the fact that the council would be unlikely to allow corporate bounty-collecting as an alternative income for the station. (A bounty probably wouldn't pay for even a week of Jolly-Baby's annual maintenance, anyway.)

I said, "Contract slavery is illegal on Preservation. You have refugee status here and no one can send you back or make you do anything you don't want to do. If I can get you back to the station." I pointed at the bag. I know, I felt like an idiot. "This is a life-tender. You're going to need to get in it."

The three humans in front, the brave ones, came forward, still afraid but desperately willing to be convinced. Human One stepped close enough to peer through the hatch, where the module's light was not being kind to my giant bag. "In that?" she said, as if honestly baffled. The others recoiled a little.

"It's not as bad as it looks," I told her. The bag had already set itself to return to the colony ship's lock and was just waiting for a go code. I wanted to pile all the humans in but the instructions insisted there was a per trip limit. I could override it, but . . . Yeah, no, better not. On the ship's feed I found cameras in engineering, the passage into the bridge, and finally, a camera pointed at the other side of the lock where the module was attached. There was no air wall, no full lock, just that round hatch. Oh, huh, I think this is a modified raider ship and that hatch is designed for ship-to-ship boarding. And there was a box attached to it that looked suspiciously like a manual release. Yikes.

(I mean, there had been an 80-plus percent chance it existed, but seeing it drove home the whole oh shit aspect of everything.)

I needed to keep telling the humans to get in the bag. "It'll hold six of you and you need to get in, now." I pointed up at the obviously rigged-for-rapid-decompression-hole in the roof of the module. "It's better than that." Was I going to have to make them get in the stupid bag? I really hoped not, because if they realized I was a SecUnit, this situation was going to go from awkward to . . . really fucking awkward. "It's self-guiding, it's a short trip, all you have to do is go through the station airlock when it opens for you."

Then Human One, still looking out at the bag, made her decision. She turned back to the others. "Come on, the youngs go first."

She picked out the three adolescents and three of the adults. There was some muffled crying and protests as she shoved them into the bag. They were afraid, they didn't want to leave the others, etc.

The bridge passage camera picked up a human in tactical gear moving past. I said, "How many aboard?"

Human One said, "We only saw two, but there has to be more. They opened the hatch once after we were locked on to look at us."

Human Two said, "They said they wanted us alive for the bounty."

Then Human Three added, "They got a SecUnit."

"They do?" Did they? I hadn't caught any pings and there's no way a SecUnit wouldn't have noticed when I took control of the ship's SecSystem. I'd had the theory that PortAuth system had been hacked by a SecUnit or CombatUnit, but that didn't fit with our current working theory that there was a local actor who had legitimate PortAuth access. "Did you see it?"

"Behind the others, in the armor," Three said. Two and Four nodded.

One made a noise under her breath and I said, "You don't think it's a SecUnit." I should have been more careful there, but I was trying to get into the ship's memory archives without waking the bot pilot, and with my drones hidden, I was mostly looking at the hatch or the bag. I wanted schematics, controls for the jury-rigged lock. No, they could still use the manual release, I couldn't jam that from here. Another hostile in tactical gear left the bridge. Yeah, I think they've alerted on me, somehow.

Human One said, "They use SecUnits up in the processing centers, not in the backrocks where we were most of the time."

When the sixth human tumbled into the bag, it signaled that it was at capacity and ready to leave. I let the module's hatch close. Then I wished I'd left a drone in the bag so I could monitor it directly. Whatever, I was just going to have to trust the damn bag.

At least I had its channel as an input and could tell it had sealed itself and scooted off to take the most direct route back to its "home" airlock. "How long will it take?" Human Three asked.

"Not long, just a few minutes," I said. If we were lucky, there would be time for a second trip and I wouldn't have to do this the hard way.

A vibration traveled through the hull and the humans flinched. "What was that?" Human Two demanded.

"They're trying to dump us!" Human Four's voice was shrill. He was right, someone in the bridge had tried (and failed, because I had control of SecSystem and it was preventing the command from going through) to release the clamps on the module. Something had spooked the hostiles and they were trying to dump the incriminating module and leave. Well, crap. Time to shift to Plan B. I connected to the station's feed and used it to send the "proceed" code to the responder. Since there was no point in hiding anymore, I also sent a feed message to Aylen and told her refugees were incoming to the colony ship.

Human One took a sharp breath. "Thanks for trying, Station Security."

Above us the ship's camera picked up a hostile in an armored suit, the one that the refugees had mistaken for a SecUnit, stepping into view of the hold camera near the jury-rigged lock above us. Oh, I get it. The hostile wasn't strong enough to activate the manual release without the armor. But I'd finally found the code they used for the jury-rigged hatch.

In one of my shows, this would have been a great time to say something brave and encouraging. I suck at that, so I said, "Get to the back of the module, on the floor, and cover your heads."

I checked my input for the life-tender; it had reached the colony ship's hull and was blorping along toward the airlock. In my peripheral vision, Human One jerked her head at the others and they scrambled toward the far end of the module. I said, "When I yell clear, I need you to follow me up into the ship."

Skeptically, Human One said, "How are you gonna—"

I pulled my explosive projectile weapon off its strap, then climbed the folded cargo rack nearest the module lock, braced my feet against the bulkhead, and held on with my free arm. As the armored hostile leaned down to reach the release, I triggered the ship's system to open the jury-rigged hatch.

It rotated open with a hiss of released air, and the module immediately smelled better.

I didn't move. The camera showed the armored hostile jerking back in surprise. A panicky yell from a hostile on the bridge came over the comm; they must have realized the bot pilot was unresponsive. But the armored hostile couldn't pull the release now, while the lock was open, without depressurizing the ship. (I'd also frozen open all the interior hatches, which, from the additional yelling over the comm, was something the bridge crew had just discovered.)

The armored hostile hesitated. Come on, look down here, you know you want to. There was going to be an orientation change between the ship's gravity field and the module's gravity field, and I'd have to take it into account. The humans huddled at the far end of the module, frozen, waiting.

The armored hostile leaned down and cautiously extended a weapon through the lock.

(I already knew it wasn't another SecUnit inside that suit, but this was another giveaway. A SecUnit would have moved fast, propelling itself into the module. There's no point in being cautious when your job is to draw fire, right?)

I woke my drones as I grabbed the armored arm and yanked it down. Twisting the hostile's weapon free and dropping it, I swung myself over to clamp my body around the armor's helmet and upper body.

I have a file of access codes I could have used to take control of the armor, but that would take time, and this was an expensive brand and might be newer than my code list. Another reason this wasn't a SecUnit—our armor was never this nice.

With my chest clamped to its helmet, Armored Hostile couldn't see and events were moving a little too fast for it to take advantage of the armor's scan, cameras, or defensive functions. I jammed the nozzle of my projectile weapon into the back neck joint where the important parts were, switched it to full power, and fired. The armor spasmed (an explosive projectile in your motor control functions will do that) and went limp.

My drones shot up through the lock and the hold, and straight into the faces of the two hostiles in tactical gear running toward us down the corridor. They screamed and flailed backward.

I climbed around the dead weight of the armored hostile and up into the ship. Then I dragged the body out of the way and yelled, "Clear!"

I took a guard position at the inner hatch and watched my drones zip through the ship. Behind me the humans scrambled to climb up through the hatch, exhausted and struggling, trying to help each other. When the last one collapsed on the deck, gasping at the fresh air, I let the lock close. That was a relief. Now that there was no more danger of everybody getting sucked into space, I checked my other inputs.

I had confirmation from the bag that it had delivered its humans to the colony ship, where the airlock had accepted its safety code and cycled them through. The responder had sent a confirmation code, and, according to the hostile ship's SecSystem, had just hailed the hostiles and informed them that they were about to be apprehended.

The armored hostile was still alive, just stunned and trapped in the immobile suit. The other hostiles were confused, panicking about the drones, and there was every chance of getting them to surrender, or at least violently encouraging them to surrender without having to kill them. To the humans, I said, "I'm going after the others, just stay here—"

I felt a hard thump from behind. It was low and to one side, where a fairly important part would be, if I was human.

I turned. Human One had the armored hostile's weapon, the one I had taken away and dropped down into the module. And she had shot me with it.

I reached her before she could fire again, twisted it out of her grip. Then I walked out of the hold and let the hatch shut behind me.

By the time the responder locked on and its armed intervention team boarded, I had the other hostiles disarmed, restrained with cuffs I'd found in a locker, and sitting on the deck near the main airlock. I'd found their medical unit (it was an off-brand model, and installed in the galley, but whatever) and was letting it seal up the hole in my back. (Just a regular projectile, not an explosive one, so most of my back was still there. I just didn't feel like walking around leaking in front of humans right now.) I'd gotten Aylen on comm and confirmed she had called in her team for support and was now trying to coax the six refugees out of the colony ship's airlock corridor. Apparently they weren't believing the whole "we're Station Security and we're here to help" story. Whatever, it wasn't my problem.

I'd switched my feed ID back to SecUnit.

Senior Indah walked in. I knew from listening to the responder's comm that she had taken a shuttle out to it, but I hadn't expected her to come looking for me. She frowned at the galley. The surfaces were smeared with dried food, and it smelled bad, even worse than human food prep areas usually smell. She looked at me and said, "You were hurt?"

I told the MedUnit to stop and pulled my shirt back down. "What gave it away?"

She folded her arms and leaned against the side of the hatch. My drones showed her expression was sour. "The refugees told me they shot you. They realized you were a SecUnit and thought . . ." She scratched her head, leaving her short hair sticking up unevenly. "I don't know what they thought, I'm too tired to sort that out. Do you want to make a criminal complaint against them?"

Uh-huh, very funny. "No." I didn't want to talk about it, so I stared at the wall. I just wanted to get off this ship, back to the station, back to my regular job making sure no one killed Mensah. "My short-term contract is completed."

"Is it?" Indah lifted her brows. "Do you know who killed Lutran?"

With everything else, I'd forgotten about the original objective of this whole mess. "No, who?"

Now she rolled her eyes. "I was asking you."

Oh, right. "But the hostiles will know who they were working with in the Port Authority."

"We questioned them briefly and they say they don't. They were given some instructions to send to a scramble-coded feed address, and they have no idea who was on the other end. We checked and the address has been deleted. I don't know if I believe they really didn't know who they were talking to, but it's going to take time to get them to realize that they can help themselves more by telling us everything." Her mouth set in a grim line. "I don't want to wait. I want to find that traitor before they do any more damage."

Did I want that too? Yes, yes I did. And the parameters of the problem had changed, drastically, in a way that made it solvable. Our suspect pool had been a bunch of humans and augmented humans wandering around in the Merchant Docks mostly unobserved and not interacting with station systems, as we tried to identify an actor who could remove themselves from the few surveillance cameras at will. Now we knew it was a local, someone with legitimate access to Port Authority systems. Locals living on the station do stuff that leaves a trail, that generates records in log files. "You need a surveillance audit."

Her frown turned confused. "A what?"

"You take all the data available during the time frame when the incidents occurred, not just from the Port

Authority systems, but from StationSec, StationComm-Central, TransportLocal, the distribution kiosks, the door systems that allow people to enter their private quarters, anything that saves an ID that tells you what someone was doing at the specific moment when we know the perpetrator was active, and you compare it to the list of potential operators to start eliminating them. It's going to be harder because your surveillance is crap, but it can still drastically reduce the suspect pool." She didn't react and I added, "If we know someone is in the station mall accessing a food kiosk at the exact time the transport suffered the catastrophic failure, then they can be eliminated as a suspect."

Her gaze turned intrigued. "Some of those systems are under privacy lock, we'd need a judge-advocate to release their access records, but the others . . ." Then she shook her head. "We narrowed down the time of death, but it's not exact. And the theory was that some of those actions, like using the cart to dump Lutran's body in the mall, were pre-arranged. The actor could have been eating in the station mall when it happened."

I explained, "But not when the transport was hacked. That can't be done over the feed. When the transport went down, the actor was there, on board."

Indah's face did something complicated, which I think

was an attempt not to show enthusiasm. "How long would this take you?"

"A few hours. And I'd need outside processing and storage space." I'd have to pull a bunch of old company code out of archive storage, build the database, and write the queries.

She pushed off the hatch. "Then let's get out of here and get started."

Chapter Eight

WE GOT ON THE responder, which had collected the refugees and the hostiles, and was now ready to leave. A station tug had already arrived and was maneuvering into position to haul the hostile ship and the module to the impound bay so they could be checked for evidence. In light of the whole traitor in the Port Authority thing, Indah had ordered the tug to keep the ship and the module in isolation until Station Security cleared it. She hadn't exactly lied, but she had implied that the ship might be contaminated with something. (Anybody who saw the galley wouldn't have any trouble believing that.)

On the quick trip back to the transit ring, I checked my feed messages. Mensah wanted me to report when I had a chance, Ratthi wanted to know if I was all right, and Gurathin wanted to know if I'd used the life-tender and if it had worked okay. I also had a report from Tural, the combined forensic/medical report, which among other things identified the cause of Lutran's death as a long "needle-like device" that had stabbed into his head, leaving no identifiable fragments behind. Tural also said the transport was being repaired, but the team hadn't managed to pull any usable data off it. And Pin-Lee's General Counsel report had arrived, which showed Lutran's name came up multiple times in regard to cargo transfer on Preservation Station and on three other allied polities. Which meant Lutran had been funneling refugees for years, through multiple stations, as we'd theorized. And he wouldn't be doing that anymore, so who the hell knew what would happen to all the other parts of the organization and the humans trapped at BreharWall-Han. I sent acknowledgments/reply laters to all of them so they'd know I was still alive, because what I really needed to do was stand here and watch the beginning of episode 132 of *Sanctuary Moon*.

I'd followed Indah to the responder's bridge, where she and the responder's captain lied to the Port Authority about what the responder was doing. (They told them that a trader ship had had an onboard emergency that caused a comm and drive failure, and that the responder had alerted because it looked like the ship was trying to break port lockdown and leave. The misunderstanding had been cleared up now and the responder was arranging to bring the ship in for repair.) (I thought it was too complicated for a good lie, but whatever.) As we docked I followed Indah down to the airlock foyer to disembark. She stopped abruptly at the top of the corridor and I didn't run into her because unlike the humans who are usually following me I pay attention. Audio picked up movement ahead; I sent a drone around the corner for a look. Oh, right, they were leading the refugees off the ship and she didn't want them to see me. Which, fine.

But standing there, I thought of something. Whoever the actor was in the Port Authority, it was a human or augmented human who thought they were pretty clever and able to manipulate systems to their advantage.

Maybe we could get them to try again. I secured a connection with Indah's feed: *I have an idea.*

She replied, *Well, your last idea didn't work out so badly. Let's hear it.*

———————

The hard part had been deciding who/what was going to be the bait. It couldn't be me; the important part (the thesis? I guess?) of our theory was that the actor was a local, with access to Port Authority if not Station Security systems. This person would know what I was and that attempting to attack me was not a good idea. (I wasn't in a great mood right now, so it was an even worse idea than it usually was.) And there had to be some explanation of how/why the bait human knew who the actor was, so it couldn't be a Station Security officer or a random station resident. I suggested Target Four from the *Lalow,* who had all the characteristics of a human who could be talked into doing anything.

Indah disagreed, on the grounds that Target Four had been talking to anybody who got within range while he was on detention in the station, and there was too high a chance that the actor would realize he didn't know anything he hadn't already told us. She thought it had to be one of the refugees, who had all had an opportunity to overhear/get information from the bounty-catchers. Which meant that even though it was my plan I couldn't be in the middle of it. Which, whatever, I didn't want to be in the middle of it where the excitement was, I wanted to be in an office working on a giant database in case the stupid plan didn't work.

For the refugee/bait, Indah chose Human Three, the one who had been convinced the armored hostile was a SecUnit. She went to talk to him with the new special investigation team she had conscripted from the responder's crew. (They had all been in the responder, which had been undocked on picket, so they couldn't have been in the transport to kill Lutran.) (The other special investigation team was still potentially compromised, except for Aylen and Indah.) (And me, I guess.)

Human Three was in the responder's medical compartment because he or someone else (I was betting it was him) had forcibly removed an interface from the skin of his forehead before leaving BreharWallHan and it had become infected. (Either the *Lalow* crew hadn't offered the use of their MedUnit or with his curly head hair flopping over the wound, they hadn't noticed.)

He was sitting on the med platform listening to Indah explain what we wanted him to do, with the other members of the new team gathered around. (I wasn't there because I'm an evil SecUnit. I was out in the responder's secure bay waiting for Indah's request for system processing space for our database to be approved, checking my inputs, pulling and sorting code out of my archive, and watching the conversation via drone.)

Human Three, hair pulled back with a big patch of new skin on his forehead, said, "I'll help you, but you got a SecUnit here. It's probably passing tales to BreharWallHan."

This would bother me more if it wasn't so fucking typical.

So it surprised me when one of Indah's conscripted responder team members said, "It was the SecUnit got you out of that module. You wanted to stay in it? It's coming with the tug, you can hop back in."

"No, no, we're not corporates, we have laws. One of which is it's illegal to put people in transfer modules so he couldn't get in it again even if he wanted to," Indah said, leaning against the bulkhead with her arms folded, as if none of this was urgent. "What we should do is charge his friend for shooting a Station Security consultant."

Human Three (whose actual name was Mish) looked uneasy. "Are you going to do that?"

Indah said, "No, because I understand she's experienced extreme trauma and because the consultant refused to make a complaint. Now are you going to work with us so we can find our killer and I can clear the *Lalow* crew and send them back to their ship? Or is this just how your whole group treats people who get hurt trying to help you?"

"I didn't say I wouldn't do it," Mish grumbled. "I just want to know why you have a SecUnit if—"

So that's how that was going.

It was the end of the day cycle and the station agencies were shutting down for their rest period, but I had asked Mensah to push through Station Security's requests. By the time Indah came out into the bay, I'd gotten a feed message that Station Resource Allotment had approved the temporary processing and storage space we'd asked for. I'd already received a notice that I now had access to StationSec and provisional access to PortAuth. We still needed to arrange data dumps from the station mall systems we could get without needing permission from the judge-advocate, but even without those I thought we had enough to get started. If I was lucky, I could at least get the original special investigation team uncompromised with the data I had so far, once I could get it into a usable form. Their help would make the bait operation easier.

Indah walked up to me, saying, "So that part's done. I just got a feed message from Aylen, she wants you over in the Security Office. The responder team will be bringing Mish with them, and I'll meet you there."

Threat assessment spiked. Huh.

I said, "So you're staying here?"

Her expression turned hard. "Not that you have any right to ask, consultant, but I need to go to the Merchant Docks and try to stand down the search teams in a way that won't alert our traitor."

"Because wandering off alone across the transit ring when we're trying to bait a murderer to act sounds like a good idea to you."

Indah glared at me. "You talk to Dr. Mensah like that?"

"Yes. That's why she's still alive."

She kept glaring. I was glaring at the air next to her head. She rubbed a spot between her eyes. "Fine. I'll bring a couple of the responder crew with me."

I waited around long enough to make sure she did. I left with them through the secure entrance and the air wall, past the access for the responder's dispatch station where I split off to cross the Public Docks toward the Security Office.

It was quiet except for the whisper of the air flow and the low hum of active energy fields. Not anomalous since the last cargo transfer had been completed hours ago and there wasn't any reason for anybody to hang around in here now. The transport crews were either on board their ships or in the station mall. It was perfectly normal and not creepy at all.

I was poking at threat assessment, trying to get a breakdown of the factors that had caused that spike. I had a lot of drone inputs sending me video and other data, but the reaction had been to what Indah said, not anything to do with Mensah's security or anything else I was monitoring. And it had spiked before I had seen how empty the Public Docks were, with the cargo bots all gone to the Merchant Docks to help with the search. Though on a normal work cycle, the cargo bots would be outside, launching and attaching modules.

Huh. We knew Lutran had arranged for his module to be launched from the Merchant Docks and directed toward the Public Docks and his transport. We knew somebody, the actor inside the Port Authority, had redirected it toward the bounty-chasers' ship. The bounty-chasers' bot pilot had picked up the module just like a raider locked onto an unarmed ship, no cargo bot needed, but Lutran's transport should have had a cargo bot assigned to help attach the module. The module's transfer records had been deleted, but the cargo bots might have a record of the request for attachment and its cancellation. Indah had gotten me provisional access, and the cargo bots' movements outside the station weren't under any kind of privacy lock, so I ran a query.

I was distracted, so it was a good thing I'd had my drones form an extra-large spherical perimeter.

The three at the sphere's apex picked up the sound of

snapping metal and gave me a .5-second warning to move. The two further out on the sphere's curve gave me an estimate of the dimensions of the falling object so I knew what direction to go in.

I threw myself out of the way and hit the metal floor in the gap between the crane's second and third arms. Nothing hit me but the sound of a heavy thing striking the floor all around and the vibration rattled the shit out of me. I'm hard to kill, but an entire hover crane landing on me would sure do it.

My drones reported no additional falling objects and I scrambled away from the crane. I used my StationSec access to kill all surveillance on the embarkation floor so whoever it was couldn't take a second shot.

I sent an alert code to the responder team and directed my drones to form a perimeter again. With nothing else heavy about to fall on me, I did what I should have done before I left the secure bay, and used the comm to call Aylen.

Farid answered, "Special Investigator Aylen can't take your call, can I help—"

"Farid, this is SecUnit, did Aylen send a feed message to Indah telling me to meet her in the Security Station Office?"

"I don't know." He sounded startled. "Maybe? She's not here yet and she's off feed for a quick break. It took forever to talk the refugees out of the colony ship's nav control and I think she just needed some personal time—"

"Find her. Make sure she's all right." Hopefully Aylen was in a restroom and not dead somewhere in a corridor. Then I signed off because my query had returned results. The cargo bot scheduled to attach Lutran's module to his transport had been cancelled by the Port Authority and directed to the opposite end of the Public Docks. Which wasn't helpful because we knew our actor was in the Port Authority so . . .

Oh. For fuck's sake, you have to be kidding me.

Pin-Lee tells me I have to make everything complicated, and wow, is she right this time.

I established a secure feed connection with Indah and said, *A crane almost fell on me in the Public Docks. Aylen didn't send you a message, someone spoofed her ID. Did you tell Supervisor Gamila about the trap?*

No! She was startled. *Of course not, I—Damn it, I told her we needed a Port Authority data dump. I had to, she had to authorize the transfer to the temp storage—It can't be her. We grew up together—*

It's not her, I said. *But I know who it is.*

I had never been in a Port Authority office before, for the same reasons I had never been in a Station Security office. But there had been a lot of firsts for me on this contract.

It was a multilevel structure, mostly private work spaces,

with the public entrance on the second level opening inward to stationside, for humans who couldn't/didn't want to do their business over the feed. There were secure entrances I could have used, but I took the public one, sending my drones zipping ahead as the transparent doors slid open. I didn't bother to remove myself from the surveillance camera at the doorway.

I did remove the responder team and the special investigation team, who were coming in through the secure dock entrance on the lower level and evacuating Port Authority workers in case a big structural-integrity-imperiling fight started.

I passed through a large open room with only two humans working with display surfaces. They looked up, startled, but I didn't stop. I walked into Supervisor Gamila's office, which had a wide curving window looking down into the Public Docks. The transparent material was interior port grade but not hatch grade. (I'd looked it up on the walk over here, along with the structure's schematic.)

Gamila sat at her desk, a half dozen documents and database results open in her feed and floating on the display surfaces around her. She was surprised to see me. Then her expression turned frightened when she saw the large projectile weapon I was holding. I said, "Run."

Balin stood beside the window, pretending to be dormant.

Gamila shoved to her feet, bumped into the desk, and bolted out the door behind me. My drone video saw her run into Aylen, who caught her and hurried her out of the office after the other workers.

I said to Balin, "The humans think you're hacked, but we both know that's not true."

Balin stood up and expanded its limbs, the top of its carapace almost brushing the curve of the high ceiling. It sent into the feed, *query: would it make a difference if I was hacked?* Then it launched a code attack to slam through my wall and hit my feed and comm connections and disrupt my processing. At the same instant it extended a limb at high speed right toward my chest.

Nice try. I deflected the code attack and stepped to the side. The limb shot through the empty air where I had been standing and punched a hole in the office partition.

My turn. I lifted my weapon and put three explosive projectiles into the center of Balin's carapace. I was hoping that would do the trick but I had a bad feeling it wouldn't. But it would still confirm my working theory.

I had run a quick check of Balin's records on the way here. It had been on Preservation Station for 43.7 local planetary years, and its original "guardian" had been the Port Authority supervisor at that time, who had taken it on when Balin jumped ship from a corporate cargo transport and asked for refuge. It had been the first and only bot to do that, which, you know, should have told the humans something.

The projectiles broke through Balin's carapace but barely dented the underlying shell. Yeah, I figured. In all its years on station, it had never requested maintenance. It couldn't, because a maintenance scan would have revealed its interior structure. Even a Preservation human would have wondered why a general-purpose bot had been fitted with military-grade armor under its outer body.

Balin dodged sideways and extended two more limbs to trap me in the corner. I ducked and rolled before another limb could pin me and fired three more bolts at its lower undercarriage. A non-standard configuration meant design flaws and gaps in its armor, and I only needed to find one.

Whatever reason Balin had originally been sent here for, nothing had ever come of it as far as I could tell from the historical search. The corporation that deployed Balin had been killed off in a takeover 27.6 years ago; its second function must have remained dormant. Until somehow BreharWallHan had ended up with its command codes and, looking for a way to plug up the pipeline of escaping contract labor running through Preservation and the other non-corporate independent polities along these trade routes, they had decided to activate it.

Possibly there had been two distinct bots in there, and Balin the general purpose bot had been erased once its secondary function had been activated by BreharWallHan. But this was why I didn't want Station Security officers in here with me: Balin's secondary function allowed it to kill humans and there is only one kind of bot made in the Corporation Rim with that function.

Under Balin's general purpose carapace, it was a CombatBot.

My second hit on its undercarriage caused it to lurch erratically. I pushed up into a better firing position and oh, that had been a trick. It pounced forward to land on me but slammed into the floor when I rolled out of the way.

It shot another limb at me and I went up the wall, fired at its extended limb joints and flipped down to land on my feet. The impacts shattered three joints before Balin slung itself around and jettisoned the broken limbs. It had more where they came from, though, and this was going to take a while. I sent, *Are you trying another code attack on me? Because I'd think a CombatBot would know the difference between a helpless transport and a SecUnit.*

I wanted to provoke it into reacting and of course it did, because it was a bot and it made mistakes, like trying to kill me when it realized the database we were building was going to show an anomalous exit and reentry through one of the outer station airlocks.

(Okay, so a human or augmented human might have made those same mistakes. Maybe exploring every possible outcome of each action in an inescapable loop of paranoia and anxiety wasn't the most normal reaction-state but hey, if it was, there would be a lot fewer stupid murders. I don't know what I'm trying to get at with this. I'd make a better corporate spy? Probably? Except not being a corporate spy left a lot more time for media so that was just never going to be an option.)

(And also, I'd rather be disassembled while conscious, again.)

I needed to get close if I was ever going to finish this, and I feinted toward the right. But Balin knew I needed to get close and decided to shift locations where it would have more room to run me down. It swung and dove for the window into the Public Docks. I'd told Station Security to keep the area clear but I had no eyes down there to make sure. So as Balin slung itself past me I grabbed a trailing limb.

I hadn't expected Balin to be able to smash through that window so fast but wow I was wrong. Falling with the shattered transparent material through the air wall and toward the transit ring floor, I jammed the projectile weapon right up against the undercarriage where Balin's lower limbs connected and fired over and over again. Then we hit the floor.

The impact knocked me off Balin and I landed two meters away. SecUnits don't stun easily and I managed to hang on to the weapon, but I'd damaged an ankle joint and struggled to get upright. Then a giant scoop thing slammed down in front of me.

For .05 of a second I had no clue what it was, then I picked up my drone inputs. JollyBaby the cargo bot had just put its hand down between me and Balin. This whole section of the ring was suddenly full of cargo bots. My drones picked up a dozen emergency medical bots, general purpose bots, even Tellus from the hostel, gathered at the public entrance on the other side of the Port Authority.

They weren't sending pings, they weren't making any noise. I had JollyBaby's hard address and sent it: *query?*

JollyBaby sent back: *Balin off network. Intruder destroyed Balin.*

For another .05 second I thought by intruder it meant me. Before the "oh shit" moment could sink in, I realized what it was actually saying.

At some point during the fight Balin had dropped its wall and its designation as a CombatBot was now open on the feed. To the other bots it looked like one moment Balin was there, and the next its body was occupied by the CombatBot. They thought the CombatBot had killed Balin. I wasn't sure they were wrong.

Balin stood there, carapace broken open, armor dented and cracked from repeated close-range projectiles, broken limbs trailing, as the other bots waited. There were no threats, no communication on the feed or comm, but the message was clear: we know what you are. None of these bots knew how to fight, but they were high functioning and would move to protect humans and each other from a violent intruder. Balin could try to fight; a CombatBot could destroy a cargo bot, no problem. But it couldn't destroy this many cargo bots plus one slightly banged up SecUnit, not all at once.

Balin's mission had depended on stealth. Now its mission was over. Its presence in the feed faded as it dropped into a resting configuration and shut itself down.

I was sitting on the platform of the Security Station's MedUnit, getting my ankle adjusted, when Senior Indah came in.

(I'd already talked to Dr. Mensah on our secure feed. She had asked if I was all right and I said yes, which was sort of true but sort of not. Mensah and Dr. Bharadwaj had been trying to think up ways to make humans less afraid of SecUnits and here was Balin, or Balin's secondary function, running around murdering humans, or a human. And Lutran's elaborate refugee escape network was cut off, leaving the current group safe on Preservation but with no idea where the rest of their people had ended up. The *Lalow* crew might try to continue their part of it, but with BreharWall-Han already on to them, they wouldn't last long. As usual Mensah didn't believe that I was all right but pretended to and said, *Why don't you come to the hotel when you're done and we'll do something fun.*

All I wanted to do was watch media and not exist. I said, *You know I don't like fun.*

Well, Ratthi has a reservation for the opening night of that new musical theater thing in Makeba Hall and he wants us all to go.

That . . . was actually really tempting. Also, guarding her in the hall would be easier if I was sitting with her. Still trying to resist, I said, *You know you don't like musical theater.*

Yes, but I like to watch other people enjoy it. Are you coming?

I gave in, said yes, and cut the connection.)

Indah said, "Good to see you in one piece."

Yeah, whatever. "You read my report?"

"I did." She added dryly, "I'm glad you documented the whole process. It's good to have a reminder that we actually didn't do too badly, except for that one basic wrong assumption."

The assumption that the perpetrator had entered the transport from inside the station instead of outside, she meant.

Balin had redirected the cargo bot in that area to the other end of the docks, then it had gone outside, walked across the station's hull, and come in through the transport's module lock and waited for Lutran. It had used the narrow rods in its hand, the rods that were part of its sealed hatch decoder, to stab him. Balin didn't have any DNA to conceal, but part of its onboard PA equipment included a hazardous materials sterilizer. It had used that on Lutran's body, to make it look like a human had killed him and had needed to remove contact DNA and any other traces left behind.

It had attacked the transport's bot pilot to cover its tracks, then it had used Lutran's ID to call the delivery cart, put the body in it, and sent it to dump it in the station mall, meaning to direct attention away from the port. Then it had returned to the station via the outside lock.

But it was a PA bot/CombatBot, not a SecUnit or a human. Its orders had been to kill Lutran, conceal its involvement, and deliver the refugees to the bounty-chasers, and that's what it had done. It could anticipate some countermeasures to its actions but didn't have the capacity to evaluate all the possible responses. And the bounty-chasers who were giving it orders hadn't anticipated the fact that Preservation Station, unused to casual or any other kind of murder, would put the port into lockdown.

Unlike Indah, I wasn't happy with our performance. Especially since I'd been the one to confuse everything by insisting the surveillance video on the transport dock had been altered. I just said, "I didn't want anything to be left to the imagination."

"Probably for the best." Then Indah sighed, and said, "I wasn't the one who sent that photo of you to the newsstreams."

It was unexpected and it made me drop some inputs. I picked them back up again. I didn't know what to say, because obviously what I should say was *I didn't think it was you* except that was absolutely not true, I had been 96 percent sure it was her.

She continued, "I wouldn't use the newsstreams like that. If we have to fight about Mensah's security, we'll fight, but I won't undermine you. Since we are actually both on the same side."

I hate being in this situation, not knowing what to say, and I couldn't even figure out a query for a search of my media archive for similar conversations because I didn't even know what kind of conversation we were having. But I didn't want to look like it had thrown me as much as it had because . . . I have no idea. The MedUnit was finished so I rolled my pants leg down and said, "I have to meet Dr. Mensah now."

Indah stepped aside as I climbed off the platform. She wasn't making an expression anymore, as if maybe she had noticed how uncomfortable I was with the conversation. Which made me more uncomfortable. She said,

"I'll authorize the hard currency card payment for you. And I assume you're open to another contract the next time something weird happens."

I paused in the doorway. The expected wave of depression at the idea of ever doing this again had somehow not happened. Huh. I said, "Only if it's really weird."

She said, "Understood."